Santa's making his list and checking it twice....

"Okay, so I'm not *really* Santa Claus. But 'round these parts, when folks think about that jolly old guy in the red suit, it's *me* they've got in mind. So I can afford to be pretty gosh-darn choosy about where I work at Christmastime—Roxanne Mercer's gift store, or Nate Carrington's catalog business."

Gonna find out who's naughty and nice...

"Now, these two darn-fool Christmas workaholics are *both* real nice—and I figure they could both use a little naughtiness in their lives. That's why I keep stringing the two of 'em along. 'Cause sooner or later they've *gotta* see what I do—that there's enough sparks flying between 'em to set a Yule log to blazing...."

Dear Reader,

Christmas is pretty much upon us, and I have to tell you, I *love* this time of year. The lights on all the trees and houses, the carols playing at the mall (because who can avoid hitting the mall at least once this season?) and especially the piles of presents and rolls of wrapping paper that start piling up in the officially designated corner of my dining room. And I have a Christmas gift for you this month, too.

Marie Ferrarella's *Desperately Seeking Twin...* is not only a terrific story about a woman finding the twin she never knew about *and* true love just in time for the holidays. It's also one part of a simultaneous duo called TWO HALVES OF A WHOLE. The other book, *The Baby Came C.O.D.*, is out right now from Silhouette Romance, so be sure to pick it up, too. You're going to love this special two-book package.

And you'll also want to buy *Seducing Santa,* a wonderful Christmas book from talented Beth Henderson. When the town's most perfect Santa fails to get hired because he's simply too good at his job, it's time for him to start giving gifts of another sort. So he takes to matchmaking and brings the gift of love to two people who are perfect for each other—and just too stubborn to see it.

Happy Holidays to you all—and don't forget to come back next year (!) for two more wonderful novels all about unexpectedly meeting, dating—and marrying—Mr. Right.

Yours,

Leslie Wainger
Senior Editor and Editorial Coordinator

Please address questions and book requests to:
Silhouette Reader Service
U.S.: 3010 Walden Ave., P.O. Box 1325, Buffalo, NY 14269
Canadian: P.O. Box 609, Fort Erie, Ont. L2A 5X3

BETH HENDERSON

Seducing Santa

SILHOUETTE YOURS TRULY™

Published by Silhouette Books
America's Publisher of Contemporary Romance

To my nieces and nephew:
Amanda, Kristin, Elizabeth,
Jessica, Lydia and Brent Daniels.
Merry Christmas to all!

SILHOUETTE BOOKS

ISBN 0-373-52058-1

SEDUCING SANTA

A Letter from the Author

There are a lot of holidays throughout the year, but the many days of Christmas are my favorites. Having worked in retail for many years, I start to get in the mood for decorating early. In the department stores, the trees and wreaths and boughs of holly are up at the beginning of November. An avalanche of catalogs appears in my mailbox about then, too. And ever since I discovered my first year-round Christmas shop, I've wanted one of my own.

In writing *Seducing Santa*, I pretty much got my wish. I have a heroine who owns such a shop, a hero who runs a holiday-theme catalog and I've got a guy who has been such a perfect mall Santa in past years, he didn't get hired this time. If the last part sounds too strange even for fiction, I've got some bad news for you. This whole story was inspired by an actual newspaper story about a Santa who was fired because he was too perfect.

Wishing you all a host of perfect Santas for the holidays and a New Year filled with romance.

Books by Beth Henderson

Yours Truly

A Week 'til the Wedding
Seducing Santa

Silhouette Special Edition

New Year's Eve #935
Mr. Angel #1002

Harlequin Historicals

Reckless #370

Prologue

In a way, the war began that day in early December when Walter Pruitt was fired. He was a big man—six-three in his stocking feet and nearly three hundred pounds. His round cheeks were ruddy, his hair was naturally white. Although he shaved for six months of the year, by the time the holidays rolled around he had always cultivated a flowing beard and mustache. He was a kind man who had a twinkle in his eye and a ready smile on his lips.

Or he did until Tot Shots, the company he'd worked for from Thanksgiving Day through Christmas Eve for the past ten years, told him they wouldn't be needing him this holiday season. They said he was *too* perfect for the job of a mall Santa. He made the other Santas look bad, which wasn't good for holiday morale. and there was nothing worse for business than a group of depressed Santas, management said. Then they added conscientiously, "Have a happy holiday."

Investigative reporters subsequently discovered that an uncle of the Tot Shots CEO had been given an ultimatum by his parole officer about getting a job, and Walter's job was the ticket to keeping the old reprobate out of the clink. However, this was all uncovered many months later and has little to do with our current story.

Marigold Pruitt, Walter's wife, was incensed at what

she considered Tot Shot's idiotic management decision in dumping her husband and called the city-desk editor at the local newspaper to tell her tale. He got hold of his best reporter and photographer and sent them hotfooting it over to the Pruitts' home.

The war broke out the morning the story hit the front page.

1

'Twas the Monday after Thanksgiving, and Nate Carrington's eyelids were at half-mast, which was their natural position at six-thirty in the morning. He'd learned to pour his first cup of coffee with them pretty well shut, but by the second cup they were generally rising in conjunction with the sun. Unfortunately, his eyelids were well ahead of his brain when it came to waking up.

He'd just finished pouring his second cup of java when the morning newspaper arrived at his house with a thud guaranteed to shorten the life expectancy of the storm door. Nate flinched and took a deep swallow of steaming black coffee before retrieving the paper. Should he call the circulation manager and complain about the method of delivery his paper carrier used? he wondered. Or should he simply bless the strength and precision the thud proved Wayne Huffman had when it came to throwing—whether the object he tossed was a rolled copy of the daily newspaper or a football? Self-interest favored the second option more than the first. He had twenty bucks riding on the accuracy of the kid's arm during the high-school game on Friday.

Nate smiled faintly as he scratched his bare chest and settled once more at the kitchen counter. Wayne was close to breaking the record he himself had set fifteen years ago as quarterback his senior year at Adams High. When the kid did, Nate planned to hand a $5,000 college scholarship check to Wayne, compliments of Carrington's Christmas Catalog. Not only would it be great local publicity for the successful business he'd built from the ground up, it would be a chance to thumb his nose at everyone who'd said he would never make it six months, much less the ten very profitable years since he'd gotten an 800 number and opened his mail-order holiday-merchandise company.

While still profitably busy, growth at the Triple C—as it was fondly called by his employees—had slowed in the past year or so. His own interest had, too, Nate admitted. He needed more than the bank of cheerful toll-free operators, more than new and exciting display and gift items to sell, more than competitive prices and guaranteed faster shipping. He needed excitement, the thrill of skunking his competition, the rush he got from making money by doing things people told him would never turn a penny.

He needed all of the above *and* an improvement in his love life.

Another once-promising relationship had gone the way of the dodo two weeks back when Pamela had called it quits. He should be used to it by now; women came and went frequently in his life. As soon as one flew off, another came fluttering around, drawn by the irresistible nectar of his success. Not that he wasn't a dashing-enough fellow to attract them without pulling his business acumen into it, but facts were facts. Women liked a man with money in his pockets. Trouble was, in the end, it was his ability to make that money that killed every relationship. Once the early glow of a romance began to dim, he tended to notice the gleam of avarice in his beloved's come-hither glance.

The breakups were rarely one-sided. While the delightful creatures enjoyed the perks his healthy income allowed, they all resented the long hours he put in to accumulate that selfsame income. Just once, he would like to meet a woman who didn't look at him with dollar signs in her pretty eyes, and who understood the demands business made on a successful entrepreneur. Such a creature was probably as mythical as old Kriss Kringle himself, but if she did exist, and he was fortunate enough to have her sashay into his life, he was grabbing hold and never letting her go. In the meantime...

The steamy vapor of freshly brewed coffee filled Nate's head, nearly clearing the last dregs of sleep away. He savored it for a moment before taking a sip, rubbing a hand along his unshaven jaw and back to knead the tense muscles at the nape of his neck. Women aside, he would be able to relax once he found a way to pump excitement back into the Triple C—maybe some gimmick to promote the catalog countrywide, year-round. He would probably sleep better, too.

Something would come to him. It always had in the past. It would now. Soon. Any minute. When he least expected it.

Like hell it would.

He hadn't had a brainstorm in months, and had been simply plodding along with business as usual. He couldn't be going stale, could he?

The coffee was strong, the shot of caffeine finally stiff enough to fully open his eyes and start the gears in his brain moving at a more even speed. Nate unrolled the newspaper, planning to put business out of his mind for the moment. He would turn to the sports section first, as usual, and find in it something that made fitting sense in his hectic world.

He never made it past the front page.

* * *

Scooping up the morning newspaper from the stoop, Roxanne Mercer tucked it under her arm and hummed "Jingle Bells" gently to herself as she fished her keys from the deep pocket of her coat. Before locking the house, she adjusted a drooping, silk poinsettia petal on the colorful wreath that hung on her front door.

The sun was topping the horizon, painting the sky in ever-warming colors. The trees had shed the last of their leaves. Birds chattered happily, perching on the newly bared limbs or among the strands of white twinkle lights Roxy had strung on her neatly trimmed evergreens. The air was brisk but not biting since winter was officially three weeks away. Roxy couldn't help but be buoyant— it was her favorite time of year.

And with good reason. December was when her Christmas-year-round shop, The North Pole Outlet, became a hive of frantic activity.

The only element missing was the promise of snow flurries. There was nothing like a touch of snow in the air to put shoppers in the mood to buy rather than browse.

Snow or no snow, Roxy was feeling wonderful. Even her in-store Santa's delayed midlife crisis, which had prompted him to take off to the Bahamas with a bubble-headed bikini queen thirty years his junior, no longer fazed her. Oh, she'd been royally ticked off with him the day before Thanksgiving when he'd called to give her the news. His timing, needless to say, stank. There wasn't a spare Father Christmas to be had this late in the season. They'd all been gobbled up by the malls, the charities, and the specialty party planners.

Still, Santa Claus's absence from her store over the Thanksgiving weekend, the biggest weekend of the year for her, hadn't been reflected in her sales figures. Did that mean she was the only one who missed having a jolly old soul in a red suit on hand? Well, if she couldn't get a Saint Nick of her own, maybe she should consider substituting with a Mrs. Claus or call a costume shop and see if they had a reindeer suit handy. She wondered whether any of her employees would step forward if she asked for a volunteer to wear antlers—probably not a one.

Since she'd expanded her shop to feature holiday bed-and-bath items, using space that had once housed back stock, the overflow of extra ornaments and wrapping paper had spilled out of the store and into her garage. For the past month she had been unable to park her sporty little Christmas-tree-green convertible inside, which meant it took a few extra minutes to let the car engine warm up—and the heater along with it—before she left for work. Still humming contentedly, Roxy slipped into the driver's seat and turned the key. She was pleased not only that the engine turned over immediately, but with the steady increase in business that made annexing her own home as a storage facility a necessity, if only temporarily.

It was very pleasant to be barely thirty and a success.

At least as far as being an entrepreneur went. Her family considered her a failure when it came to personal relationships. Her sisters had leaped wholeheartedly into marriage, snagging husbands before their twenty-first birthdays. Roxy had yet to convince them that The North Pole Outlet was as important to her as their mates and children were to them. The business certainly ranked higher than any of her former boyfriends ever had. Not that there had been many of them. She'd always put financial gain above emotional gain, even as a child—a direct result, her college roommate had told her while in the hypnotic grip of Psychology 101, of the ups and downs of her parents' income when she was at an impressionable age.

Whether that was the reason she strove for financial security or not, Roxy had to admit things hadn't been easy while she was growing up. Her father's income as an indifferent furniture salesperson working on commission had kept the family bouncing from feast to famine—near famine being the more common situation. Her mother's receptionist job hadn't added much to the family coffers, which meant raising four girls had been a shoestring affair.

While her siblings had spent their allowances on candy, and later on cosmetics, Roxy had become the first Mercer child to open a savings account. She'd had enough in it to transfer over to a more profit-building CD on her fifteenth birthday. At sixteen she had taken a full-time job after school; at seventeen she had won a full academic scholarship to college; and at twenty-one, with a degree in business, she had already parlayed her savings into a sizable sum. It was then that she'd stunned everyone by risking her money in opening not just a business of her own, but a business linked to a single holiday. Roxy had never regretted the decision, and had the sports car and a four-bedroom ranch house to prove that gambling on Christmas had been a very smart decision.

Success was a nebulous thing, though. She'd achieved all the goals she'd set, and even some beyond the original ones. Now she felt it was time to take the next step. All she had to do was figure out what direction she wanted to go with that step. Her family continued to lobby for a romantic "happily ever after"—something she became less sure existed as the years went by and her sisters debated whether or not to divorce their once-prized spouses.

Besides, Roxy reasoned, she hadn't met a man in a long

time who even caught her eye, much less had the ability to knock her socks off. Until one came along, she would stick to business.

She'd been putting off making new projections for the coming year, using the holiday season as the excuse. Even that would be over before she knew it, so while her staff of ten ''elves'' settled into taking inventory in January, she would have to make the decision to either buy out the lease of the travel agency next door so she could expand her current space, or open a second store across town.

Undecided over whether to think about the Claus vacancy or a new business plan while waiting for the car to warm up, Roxy did neither and opened the newspaper.

Fate made the decision for her. The ruddy-cheeked man in the red suit pictured above the front-page fold looked both stunned and lost.

And absolutely perfect.

Roxy changed the tune she was humming and reached for her cellular phone. It was only when her call was answered that she broke off singing ''Santa Claus Is Coming to Town.''

Walter Pruitt and his wife lived in a quiet but pretty little neighborhood, Nate decided as he unfolded his six-foot-one frame from behind the wheel of his holly-berry-red Corvette. Parking in the area, though, was the pits. He'd finally found an empty spot at curbside a block away on the narrow street and only hoped that his paint job wouldn't end up scratched while he was away from the car.

After sloshing coffee over the kitchen counter earlier as he'd read the headline—Santa Pink-Slipped!—the brainstorm he'd longed for had hit. He hadn't wanted to wait until he reached the office to set his executive assis-

tant on Pruitt's trail, so he'd spent ten minutes letting the
phone ring before Ava deigned to answer it at home. Then
it had taken a bribe—the use of the family time-share
condo in Florida the week between Christmas and New
Year's Day—before she agreed to drop her seven-grain-
muffin breakfast and do his bidding before 8:00 a.m. If
she wasn't so damn efficient, he wouldn't put up with her
demands.

Which was a lie. Even if she hadn't been efficient, he
would have given her whatever she wished. Ava was
nearly twice his age and had been with him since his first
year in business. In giving him the benefit of her twenty-
five years' experience in the mail-order business, she had
taught him more about running the Triple C than he'd
ever learned from the management courses he'd taken in
college. He would really miss her when she followed
through on one of her threats and actually retired.

Ava wasn't ready for a less hectic life quite yet. She
had a new boyfriend and fancied herself madly in love—
for the fifth time in her life, she claimed—so Nate knew
offering the carrot of the condo as a romantic getaway
would tip the scales in his favor. Besides, the condo would
be empty until after the New Year anyway, and for being
the miracle worker she was, Ava deserved a special reward.

She'd earned it, too, coming up not only with the de-
posed Santa's number and address as requested, but with
an appointment for Nate to speak to him that same day.

Nate checked his watch. He would have to hustle to
make it to Pruitt's door on time. Still he lingered a moment, retrieving his briefcase, smoothing down his neck-
tie—a tasteful repeat pattern of tiny sleighs and soaring
reindeer—checking his appearance in the reflection of the
tinted windows as he locked the car and engaged the

alarm. Since the Triple C did business only by phone, he usually wore running shoes, jeans and a sweatshirt. He was glad he'd taken the time to unearth his seldom-worn, charcoal-gray three-piece suit, although canceling the long-delayed haircut last week had most definitely been a mistake. Nate brushed at the flyaway strands of sandy hair that stuck out over his ears.

It was an easy matter to lengthen his stride to make up time. Glancing at the house numbers, he pinpointed the Pruitts' abode as the Cape Cod with the white picket fence. It looked well-kept. That could work for him or against him when it came to wheeling and dealing. He would have to feel Santa's double out to know how little moola he could get away with offering to have Pruitt work for him. Judging by the photo that had appeared in the newspaper that morning, he figured Walter could be easily turned back into a jolly old soul, which in turn would make him the perfect cover model for Carrington's Christmas Catalog, and an even more perfect sales representative to visit holiday specialty shops year-round. Who, after all, wouldn't want to buy their ornament and tinsel stock from Santa Claus?

Nate could almost see the mountain of orders that would result from adding Walter Pruitt to his full-time staff.

It was a pretty day, a day geared toward success, so Nate wasn't surprised in the least when the most gorgeous woman he'd ever seen rounded the corner from the side street and strode directly toward him. Her hair was a russet color that rivaled autumn leaves. It fell in soft waves to her shoulders. Her delightful form was only partly disguised by an ankle-length, unbuttoned, tailored, camel-color wool coat. Beneath it she wore something in navy— whether suit or dress Nate didn't know or care. He was too entranced by the vision of long, shapely legs shown to advantage by her short, slimly cut skirt and high-heeled navy pumps. Her purse mimicked a briefcase in design and swung from a long strap slung over her right shoulder. The bag bulged slightly.

As she got closer, he was able to admire the perfection of her features, each enhanced carefully with profession- ally applied makeup. It was a toss-up which he liked best—her deep red lips or her intelligent, gorgeous green eyes. Gazing into the latter over a candlelit meal had ap- peal; tasting the former had even more.

They arrived before the Pruitt house at the same time; reached for the gate in unison.

Nate moved back a step, gallantly gesturing her through before him. Good, he thought. She was obviously there to sell Mrs. Pruitt cosmetics, which would keep his future employee's spouse conveniently out of the room.

Success would soon be his.

Roxy's gaze swept over the man swiftly, taking in the excellent cut of his dark suit, the steadiness of his smile, the polite yet slightly superior way he motioned for her to precede him down the Pruitts' front walk. He was an attractive fellow and obviously new to his job. While his suit fit beautifully, he was in desperate need of having his slightly wavy, sandy-blond hair styled. He'd probably spent every penny he had at the tailor's, little realizing that grooming also mattered. What type of employment had him calling on Mr. and Mrs. Pruitt? Door-to-door en- cyclopedias, brushes, magazines? No, he hadn't stopped anywhere else on the street that she had seen. And she'd certainly followed every one of his loose-limbed strides closely, drawn by the masculine beauty of each step.

This wasn't the time to be attracted to a man, she silently reproached herself. She hadn't gotten where she was by putting a man, no matter how handsome he was, ahead of her business.

Besides, he, too, was here on business. Her eyes dropped to his briefcase as they both mounted the porch steps. If not encyclopedias or magazines, then it must be life insurance he was pushing.

"Allow me," he insisted smoothly and leaned on the doorbell.

He had a nice voice, deep and comforting. He had nice eyes, too. Gray ones fringed with lashes that were far too long and lush to belong to a man. Yet that was most definitely what he was—and a predatory one, at that. She could sense it in the slight curve of his lips as he looked down at her more diminutive form, making no effort to hide the fact that he was chronicling each of her physical assets.

Roxy didn't mind. Surreptitiously, she did the same to him. No matter what he was selling, he was without a doubt the sexiest door-to-door salesman she'd ever run across.

The door was opened by a tall, large-boned woman. Her hair was cut short, far shorter than the shaggy-haired insurance guy's, and was an attractive combination of gray and black. Her clothing was casual—coffee-colored slacks and matching boat-neck pullover. As she pushed the front storm door open, the late-morning light caught and burnished the long, carefully wrought metal necklace that lay on her generous bosom.

The smell emanating from the house was more impressive than the woman. It was a mixture of chocolate, molasses, vanilla, pine and cherry scents melding perfectly together. Roxy could almost see them, and found herself lifting her nose in appreciation of the tantalizing vapors.

If Santa Claus really did exist, his home at the North Pole would smell exactly like the Pruitts' home.

"Yes?" the woman said.

Roxy came back to earth. "Mrs. Pruitt? I'm Roxanne Mercer. I believe I'm expected?"

"And I'm Nate Carrington," the salesman added in quickly. "I have an appointment with Mr. Pruitt."

With Pruitt! Roxy frowned at him, determined to no longer find him as attractive as she had a moment before. Unfortunately he chose that moment to up the wattage of his smile, nearly knocking from her mind the reason why she was on the Pruitts' doorstep. The ingrained habit of putting business first kept her from becoming too dazed.

Roxy drew herself up, trying to make her petite form more imposing. "As do I," she said. "For eleven, which it is now." She looked the salesman in the eye. "You must have mistaken the time."

"Have I?" he asked, sounding entertained by her statement rather than confused. "More likely you've mistaken the date. My appointment is for today at eleven."

Not willing to budge an inch, Roxy squared off against him, unconsciously lifting her chin in a challenge. "As is mine," she declared.

"Now, children," the woman in the doorway chided gently. "Don't be naughty. Be nice. You're both right. Since you called within minutes of each other, Wally decided to see you together rather than separately."

Now why would Pruitt do such a thing, Roxy wondered, when he knew that she planned to offer him employment and the obnoxious creep standing next to her was only going to try to sell him something? Unless—

What had the cretin said his name was? Carrington? Why did that sound familiar?

Too quickly the answer came to her. Oh, no. It couldn't

be. Not *Carrington's Christmas Catalog!* They were one of her own suppliers. They couldn't want to hire her personal Father Christmas away! It didn't matter that she'd considered having a substitute character fill in this year. The truth of the matter was, the season just wouldn't feel right without a Kriss Kringle in her shop. And, according to the newspaper article, Pruitt was so perfect in the role it would be a crime to let him slip away to a competitor—especially one who didn't have a retail outlet.

When Mrs. Pruitt stepped back from the door, inviting them both inside the house, Roxy made sure she slipped in a step ahead of her now despised rival. She wasn't sure whether Carrington let her precede him out of innate courtesy or because letting her shove ahead of him made her appear rather pushy.

Probably the latter. Or so it seemed when she glanced back and caught a supercilious grin riding his lips. It wouldn't be there for long, Roxy vowed. Hiring Walter Pruitt meant too much to her to lose him in a hiring war to Carrington. Although she had yet to meet the pink-slipped Saint Nick, she would offer whatever incentives it took to have this particular Mr. Kringle at her North Pole—only instead of just for the season, she would offer him the plum of year-round employment, something her former Santa had always shunned when it was suggested.

The main thing was to hire Pruitt as soon as possible, not only so that he could entertain the kiddies while their parents shopped in her store, but for the free publicity to be gained when the newspaper followed up on his new situation. Upon reading a second story, a whole new segment of Santa-sympathetic customers would be brought to her door.

With visions of sales figures dancing in her head, Roxy

was a microsecond off her stride when Walter Pruitt rose from his chair to greet his visitors.

Carrington's hand jetted out, his longer reach guaranteeing that he gripped Pruitt's hand first. "Mr. Pruitt? Nate Carrington. Thank you for agreeing to see me on such short notice."

"Not at all, not at all," Pruitt declared, his deep voice managing to sound jovial despite his recent firing from Tot Shots. He pumped Carrington's arm, but Roxy was pleased to note that his bright eyes strayed to her more petite form.

Pruitt was a giant of a man in height as well as breadth. Although Nate Carrington was tall and broad-shouldered, his lean form was practically dwarfed by the man who would be Santa. At barely five foot five, Roxy felt much as she had as a child in a room full of adults—overwhelmed. Not only did the men tower over her, Mrs. Pruitt topped her by nearly six inches.

She wasn't a child any longer, though. She was a determined and, if need be, ruthless businesswoman. Roxy squared her shoulders and offered Pruitt her hand, letting him take the necessary step forward to shake it. "And I'm Roxanne Mercer of The North Pole Outlet. I believe I mentioned on the phone earlier that I'd like you to be my Santa this year." There, she thought, that should trim Carrington's sails. She'd gotten her offer on the table first.

When she glanced over at him, Carrington looked far from trimmed. In fact, he looked more as if he was running at full sail ahead of a fair wind and had no intention of altering his course.

He chuckled. "I would think a good number of men would be willing to be *your* Santa, Ms. Mercer. Wouldn't you agree, Mr. Pruitt?"

Roxy fumed silently. Trust a man to put a sleazy interpretation on her words. At least he hadn't offered to let her sit on his own lap.

He looked as if he wanted to suggest it, though.

Five minutes earlier and she wouldn't have minded complying, either. But now...

"Please make yourselves at home," Mrs. Pruitt urged. "Can I take your coat, Ms. Mercer? Get anyone a cup of hot cocoa? Wally and I were just about to indulge."

"I'd love one," Carrington declared.

He'd probably accepted just to make her look bad if she turned the offer down, Roxy thought as she slipped out of her coat. She smiled at her hostess as she handed it over, then sank gracefully onto the overstuffed sofa. "Yes, please. It sounds perfect."

"Marigold's own recipe," Walter declared proudly as his wife left the room and he settled back into his recliner. "Not a bit thin and watery like the stuff you get out of a package or in the restaurants. She makes it with steamed whole milk and—"

As she saw her carefully watched diet wash away in a flood of high-calorie, high-fat-content ingredients, Roxy's resentment of Nate Carrington grew. If he hadn't been there, she could have declined without appearing to insult her hosts.

"Sounds like a recipe worthy of Mrs. Claus herself," Carrington said, oozing charm.

"I've often told her that myself," Pruitt agreed.

Roxy searched her mind for something both witty and complimentary to say and came up dry. Should she offer to help Marigold Pruitt in the kitchen? It was the polite thing to do, but if she followed the decrees laid down in her mother's lessons in manners, Carrington would no doubt take advantage of her absence and get Walter's signature on the dotted line. She couldn't let that happen.

Besides, she was here on business and certain standards had to be maintained. She wouldn't have felt required to rush to assist Mrs. Pruitt had the woman been an office secretary who'd offered to get coffee. Despite the logic, Roxy fidgeted.

Should she compliment Pruitt on his home? To do so and sound enthusiastic would be difficult. While the Pruitts obviously considered their house cozy, their decorating was far from a designer's dream. As befitted the couple, the furniture was large scale and thus crowded the room. The walls were covered with dark paneling and nearly free of decoration. A lone landscape hung over the sofa, its theme a moon-washed beach—not exactly the type of setting one associated with a Santa, even a pseudo-Santa. A cuckoo clock shaped like a tiny Swiss chalet hung above the twenty-four-inch console television. A handmade afghan of colorful granny squares was folded over the back of a wing chair. On the floor nearby, a basket of yarn and partially crocheted squares showed that another throw was in progress. Walter Pruitt's wide recliner sat to the right, a rack of lovingly kept pipes displayed on the table next to it. All the furniture was arranged to face the television screen. Roxy itched to add more life to the room. It was only when she closed her eyes and concentrated on the heavenly aroma that filled the house that the Pruitt home took on a personality.

Whereas she had trouble finding a subject to talk about other than the one that had brought her to the Pruitts' front door, Nate Carrington appeared to have no such problem.

"Personally," he said, "it's memories of my grandmother's fudge that say Christmas to me." He took a seat next to Roxy on the sofa, resting his right ankle on his left knee, totally at ease in his surroundings.

Despite her resolve to keep her mind on business, Roxy

couldn't help being very aware of him. As Carrington leaned back against the cushions, the sofa springs seemed to tilt her lighter form toward his. Although she carefully put another two inches of space between them, she still felt the warm, comforting heat of his body and smelled the sensual scent of his aftershave.

"Christmas wouldn't be Christmas without fudge," Pruitt remarked. "Was it dark or light chocolate?"

"Neither. Peanut butter," Carrington answered.

Roxy didn't know how he did it, but just the way he said those two words had her mouth watering.

"She used to bundle pieces of it up in holiday napkins and tie them closed with a piece of curled ribbon. Never expected to get a lump of coal in my stocking but, boy, if I didn't get one of those packages of fudge I knew I'd gone wrong of Grandma somehow," Carrington said. "What about you, Ms. Mercer?"

Deep in contemplation of the smell and taste of fresh, fattening and forbidden peanut-butter fudge, Roxy started when he addressed her. "Me?"

"Any special goodies that say Christmas to you?" Carrington asked.

She was amazed that he sounded sincere.

Pruitt was more so. "Let me guess," he said as he took a pipe from the rack at his side. "Rolled sugar cookies that you helped cut out and decorate."

Roxy watched as Pruitt tapped a bit of fresh tobacco into the bowl of his pipe. No wonder the house smelled right to her. He used cherry-scented tobacco. It had been a long time since she'd been enveloped in that particular sweet aroma.

"Actually, no," she said and grinned fondly at the memory that surfaced in connection with the scent of

Pruitt's newly lit pipe. "What I remember best are the bags of pennies."

"Pennies?" Nate Carrington echoed with faint surprise.

Forgetting for the moment that she was determined to dislike him, Roxy leaned forward in her seat and favored Carrington, as well as Pruitt, with a genuine smile. "Yes. You see," she explained, "my great-grandfather smoked a pipe like you do, Mr. Pruitt. One of his brands of tobacco—I don't know which—came in small muslin bags with drawstring tops. He saved them throughout the year, and come Christmas he'd fill the bags with pennies and hide them around his living room. When we came to visit, my sisters and I always knew we'd have a treasure hunt and come away fifty cents richer." If Carrington hadn't been paying such close attention, she might have gone on to confess that she still had the last bag of pennies she'd found. Her great-grandfather had died two days before Christmas the year she was ten, but he'd managed to leave the annual treasure behind for the children. It was the only batch of pennies that she had never put to work for her in the bank.

"What a lovely idea," Mrs. Pruitt commented as she reentered the room, a tray of steaming mugs in her hands. She set the tray on top of the television set and handed the stoneware cups of cocoa around before taking a seat in her wing chair. "But, do you know, I don't think any of your tobacco comes in anything other than a plastic bag, Wally. It looks like progress has killed yet another family's tradition."

Considering it had been twenty years since the last treasure hunt, Roxy doubted progress should take the heat over the demise of this tradition. Besides, now that she'd shared it with the Pruitts—and Carrington, of all people!—she didn't particularly want outsiders adopting her great-grandfather's specialty. It was hers to cherish along with his memory.

Carrington saved her from making a comment. "Mmm. You're quite right, Pruitt. This is the best hot chocolate I've ever tasted."

Although she didn't look like the type of woman who blushed easily, Mrs. Pruitt colored up prettily. "You're being kind, Mr. Carrington," she insisted.

"Nate," he said. "Carrington's too much of a mouthful."

"We're Wally and Goldy, then," Pruitt declared.

When all eyes turned toward her, Roxanne hastily swallowed a gulp of cocoa and murmured, "Roxy."

"All right, then," Wally said. "Since I already know what you two kids want for Christmas, and you both can't have me, why don't you each lay your cards on the table and see what turns up?"

Relieved that the conversation would now be solidly on business, Roxy relaxed a bit. She'd never been good at socializing, but she was very good when it came to wringing a deal out of a supplier. That skill would stand her in good stead now.

Guile would work even better.

"That's an excellent idea, Wally," Roxy said, cradling her mug between her hands. "In the spirit of holiday giving, I'm going to let Carrington's Christmas Catalog make the first offer. The floor is all yours, Nate."

2

So much for guile, Roxy thought as she stood on the porch listening to Walter Pruitt shut the door behind her. He and his wife had listened attentively while Nate had given his pitch, offering a salary of ten dollars an hour and a job scope that Roxy felt sounded a lot more substantial and long-term than what she had to offer. Neither of the Pruitts had said a word when he finished but had turned as one to face Roxy, patently expecting her to top Carrington's deal. Which she had by throwing caution to the winds and asking Wally to play Santa all twelve months of the year for a whopping annual salary of twenty-two thousand. She hoped the gross income sounded like a lot more than Nate's offer, although in fact, it was barely ten-percent more. It had taken some fast mental math on Roxy's part to come up with the figure, yet it hadn't appeared to impress the Pruitts. Thanking the pair of eager employers for stopping by, Walter and Marigold had insisted the two offers bore thinking on and said they would be in touch.

It sounded an awful lot like "Don't let the door hit you on your way out." Not encouraging.

Next to her on the stoop, Nate sighed deeply and shoved his hands into his trouser pockets, bunching up his suit jacket in the process. "So much for that, hmm, Roxy?"

"Mmm," she answered noncommittally.

"You topped my offer nicely," he said. "I'm a little surprised Wally didn't bite at a job that was clearly little work for higher pay."

She'd been surprised herself but wasn't about to let Carrington know that. "Only time will tell," she murmured and glanced at her watch. "It's been nice meeting you, Nate, but I've got to get back to the shop. We're into the busy season, you know."

"Right," he agreed. "You run shy on anything, give Triple C a call. I'll make sure you get your order the next day, if not sooner. We're right in the same town, after all."

"Thank you," Roxy said. He made no mention of waiving the express service charge that would be tacked on to her bill should she take him up on the offer. Well, he was a businessman. What did she expect? "I'll keep that in mind," Roxy promised, knowing quite well that there would be no reason for her to call. After seven years in business, she knew almost to the piece how much to order for the shop and had arranged to have all her shipments in long ago. Her next order with Carrington's Christmas Catalog was probably months away from being placed. It would not demand express-service delivery.

They parted at the gate, the same place they had met. Roxy turned right; Nate turned left. A glance back along the street as she settled behind the wheel of her convertible showed Roxy his tall form bent, a frown marring his attractive features as he examined the paint on the bumper of an expensive red sports car.

Men and their cars, she thought in amusement, and patted the dashboard of her own vehicle. "Sorry we can't put the top down, old thing," she told the convertible, "but we're talking fairly frozen-tundra temperatures here. Never fear, though. Spring will come again." She fancied the engine purred happily at the news. At least something was happy.

Letting the car idle, Roxy picked up her cellular phone to check how things were going at the shop. "North Pole Outlet," a cheerful voice answered. "Blitzen speaking."

Roxy grinned in amusement. So the sales team had actually opted to identify with Santa's reindeer rather than his elves. She'd thought they'd been joking when they suggested it at the staff meeting, but whatever it took to keep them buoyant during this exhausting season was fine with her. "Blitzen, huh? I thought you had decided to be Dasher, Bridget."

"I was until that party I went to last night, Rox. Believe me, I'm totally incapable of *dashing* much today," the head clerk said. "Seems like an excellent time to exercise some of that delegating you've been urging me to try."

"So things are moving smoothly?"

"Like a dream," Bridget assured. "How'd things go with the jolly old soul?"

"He's thinking about joining us."

"Only thinking?"

"Mmm," Roxy said. "I'm going to grab a bite of lunch before returning. Anybody need anything while I'm out?"

"The vote was for pizza delivery, so we're fine, boss. Take your time," Bridget urged.

It was all well and good for her chief of staff to subtly suggest she take some time off, but doing so was nearly impossible. Work had become a habit Roxy was unlikely to break, especially during the holiday season. She would swing by a fast-food franchise and order a salad and a low-calorie soft drink. Within ten minutes she would be on her way back to the store, as Bridget knew quite well.

Her mind already on the things she had planned to accomplish that day, she was surprised when a streak of red whipped by her on the cross street. Carrington's Corvette. He would get pulled over and read the riot act for driving too fast in a residential area, but what did she care? A hefty fine would take him down a peg or two, she thought as she pulled out onto the street and took the turn, falling in behind the blur that was Carrington's car. Could be the consequences of a ticket would even keep him so occupied that he would be unable to contact Walter and Marigold Pruitt again. Now *that* would be a decided plus. Roxy didn't plan to let much time elapse before she called the couple again. Time was of the essence.

Ahead of her, the scarlet car pulled into a convenience-store lot. The driver's-side door opened and slammed shut again as Nate legged it over to a pay phone.

Now, why…? Oh, hell!

Roxy grabbed her cellular phone and one-handedly punched in the necessary numbers. A glance to where Nate stood showed him barely a second behind her in placing his call. One to the same number, if she read the man correctly.

Relief swept over her when there was the sound of ringing on the line. "Hello?" a woman's voice answered after the third ring.

Roxy pulled over to the side of the road, glancing quickly toward the pay phone where she saw Carrington fuming as he hooked a finger in the cradle and retrieved his quarter for another try. "Goldy? This is Roxy Mercer again. I know it's only been a few minutes since I left, but I was wondering if you and Wally would like to have a tour of The North Pole Outlet while you consider my offer. That way, if you have any questions, we could talk further. You would? Lovely. When? Whenever you'd like.''

Over in the convenience-store lot, Nate looked as if he was tempted to rip the phone from the glass enclosure. Fuming, he gathered up his returned coin once more, his gaze drifting to the curb where Roxy was parked, the motor of her car still running. Even from a distance she could see his brow knit over the bridge of his nose when he spotted her sitting in her car, phone in hand. He knew to whom she was speaking, just as she'd known whom he was about to call. It felt great to have beaten him, even over such a small thing as a phone call.

Roxy's spirits soared even higher when Marigold Pruitt made a suggestion. ''Tomorrow afternoon?'' Roxy repeated. ''That would be perfect. I'll see you both at three, then.''

It was impossible to keep the wide, superior smile from her face. Beaming broadly, she slipped the cellular back in the phone rest and waved cheerily at Nate. Just before she pulled back into the flow of traffic, she gave in to temptation and made a gesture guaranteed to rile Nate Carrington even more.

Nate stood cemented in place as Roxanne Mercer cruised slowly by in the conservatively toned dark green convertible. She looked awfully good with her cheeks reddened by the brisk air. Against the soft camel wool of her coat, her hair looked as burnished as Goldy Pruitt's jewelry. She was the kind of woman a man was willing to follow to the ends of the earth. Or at least around town until she sicced the police on him. The smile Roxy gave him was triumphant rather than a come-on, but he only realized he was in trouble when she licked the tip of one elegant, tapered finger and marked a giant 1 on an invisible scoreboard.

So, the minx wanted war, did she? Although it went against the grain to undermine one of his customers—he would have to check the records when he got back to the office to find out just how good a Triple C customer Roxy was—when it came to which one of them would get Pruitt in the end, he intended to be the winner. So what if she was ahead, or thought she was, at the moment? How many football games had he played in where the score went against his team until the last quarter? Lots.

The game wasn't over until the clock ran out, which it would only do when Santa signed on the dotted line—with Carrington's Christmas Catalog, naturally.

It wouldn't do to call Pruitt hot on Roxy's heels. He needed to come up with a plan of action first. A step-by-step campaign with enough built-in features to riposte that delectable-looking redhead at every turn.

The phone receiver was still clutched in his left hand. His quarter lay warming in his right. Nate stared at both for a moment, then slipped the coin into the slot on the pay phone and dialed the number of his private office. "Ava, darling," he greeted his miracle-working assistant when she answered. "Don't pack for Florida just yet. I've got a new assignment for you."

Wally Pruitt looked at his wife as she put the phone receiver carefully back in its cradle. "I know that expression, buttercup," he warned her. "You're up to something."

"Am I?" Goldy reached over and laid her hand over his for a moment before settling back in her chair and resuming the crochet work that Roxy's call had interrupted. "I suppose that I can't keep anything from you after all these years."

He snorted at the idea. "I'm not omnipotent. I may have the knack of knowing when children are naughty or nice, but I still can't read your mind, so you'd better let me in on your plan."

"Plan?" she repeated innocently. "What makes you think I'm plotting anything?"

"Nothing but that particularly pleased smile of yours," he said.

She sighed but she didn't stop grinning. "What did you think of our visitors?"

"Nice couple of kids," he allowed, wondering where his wife was going with this particular line of questioning.

"Were you tempted by either of their offers?"

It was his turn to grin. "Were you?" he asked, then laughed. "No, don't answer. When it comes to this, I do know your mind, just as you know mine."

She hooked a series of chain stitches, feeding the yarn by rote. "Yes, I do," she agreed. "All I ask is that you don't give either of them an answer just yet."

"Ah, you *are* scheming," he said.

"It isn't scheming," she insisted. "It's simply giving them a shove in the right direction. They were obviously made for each other."

"You don't say," he murmured.

"As much as we were meant to be together," she said. "You do agree that we are a perfect couple, don't you?"

Wally made a production of refilling his pipe. "After as long as we've been married, I've learned better than to think any differently."

Goldy reached over and swatted his knee playfully. "Oh, you," she chided. "Roxy and Nate have the same thing in common that we do. They love Christmas."

Wally nodded wisely before lighting his pipe. "That they do," he agreed. "That they most definitely do."

Roxy looked up as Bridget stuck her head around the open door of the office the next day. "We're living under a lucky star, you and I," the head clerk announced.

Having gone over her account book to see just how much she could, if necessary, raise her salary offer to Walter Pruitt, Roxy wasn't inclined to agree with Bridget. "How so?"

Rather than enter the room, Bridget leaned casually in the doorway. "No one's called in sick with the flu, and we finally filled the last Christmas-help opening."

Roxy frowned. "I thought we had hired all the help we needed."

"Had until one of them called in to quit a little while ago," Bridget said. "But I'd hardly hung up the phone when the sweetest, most grandmotherly lady walked up to the counter and asked if we had any temporary openings. She said she was interested in making extra money so she could redo her whole Christmas tree in Radko ornaments. How could I not hire a woman with such great taste?"

Or at least with expensive taste, Roxy mentally amended. She wilted back in her padded desk chair. "I suppose we should feel fortunate."

Bridget hooked a stray strand of dark brown hair behind her ear. "Trust me. You'll love Ava," she said.

When Roxy still didn't look happy with the situation, the head clerk sighed. "Listen, if it doesn't look like she's going to work out, we'll let her go before it's too late. Okay?"

"I suppose," Roxy agreed. "When was the other temp supposed to start?"

"Er, today?"

"When today?"

"At three."

Roxy groaned. "Why must everything happen at three today?"

Bridget pushed free of the door molding. "Never fear. I'll keep the new elf out of your way when Saint Nick and his missus are here. I'll have her start at the register with me."

"Okay." Roxy was about to go back to her ledgers when she noticed the name badge Bridget was wearing. Vixen, it read. "I thought you were answering to Blitzen," she said, indicating the pin on Bridget's cherry-red bib apron.

"That was before this really cute guy came in," Bridget explained. "But all he wanted was directions to the nearest toy store. About half an hour ago, another gorgeous hunk strolled in and he's still out there browsing. I thought it might be wise to change my name to give him the right impression. Unlike you, fearless leader, I don't intend to be single all my life."

Before Roxy could comment, her chief elf vanished back to the sales floor. Now where, Roxy wondered, had Bridget gotten the idea that she never intended to marry? Such was not the case at all, even if she rarely had a date. For that matter, she rarely met any eligible men. There were one or two she had seen at chamber-of-commerce meetings and subsequently had dinner with, but business matters always managed to arise when it came to making plans for a second date. Business was a wonderful excuse for her—unfortunately, it was for the men, too.

More likely, Bridget had bought her mother's act the last time she had stopped by the shop to regale everyone with stories about Roxy's sisters' children. The hints that

Roxy herself should be supplying a grandchild or two were always less than subtle.

To make her mother ecstatic it took finding a man she could like as well as love, and they were few and very far between—especially when it came to the "like" part.

Too bad about Nate Carrington. She had a feeling she could *like* him; like him a lot.

But since he was her rival over Walter Pruitt, that wasn't possible. Or at least it wasn't possible on a social level. When they next met—if they met—it would be nothing less than open warfare between them.

Which was a shame.

Roxy sighed softly over the what-might-have-been dream, then picked up her pencil once more, resigned to rechecking her figures. It was just possible she could go as high as five hundred a week for Pruitt. She would have to find something more for him to do besides talk to children for that kind of salary. While the store sold Christmas decorations year-round, only a handful of kids tagged along with their parents for eleven of those months. She'd gotten carried away in declaring the job of Santa was a full-time position. Pruitt would only need to play Santa on Saturdays and during their annual Christmas-in-July sale. Could such a large man handle the delicate ornaments while engaged in stockkeeping duties, or would his size make him more of a bull in her china shop? It bore thinking about, but first she had to keep Pruitt from falling into Nate Carrington's clutches.

And if she couldn't? It didn't bear thinking on, Roxy decided, as she closed the account book. She had to emerge the winner. But until Wally handed her a signed W-4 slip, she couldn't discount the possibility that Nate would come up with a better, more alluring offer and seduce Santa into working for him.

She could easily make herself crazy trying to guess how Nate's mind worked. It was much more productive to take a run through her own shop to make sure everything was perfect before the Pruitts arrived. This particular Santa and his spouse needed to be impressed with The North Pole Outlet. *Very* impressed.

All was not well on the sales floor.

At first glance it looked perfect, a winter wonderland. A ten-foot artificial balsam fir's limbs dipped beneath the weight of shimmering Jack Frost-white ornaments, a thousand tiny twinkle lights and artistically draped, wired, gold-mesh ribbons. Baskets of similar ornaments and ribbon nestled beneath the boughs for easy selection. Other trees, some smaller, some wider, were scattered around the huge barnlike room, each with a separate theme—one of delicate papier-mâché angels, one of cloth dolls and wooden country hearts, one of handblown Radko ornaments, one of metallic suns, moons and stars.

Overhead the rustic posts and beams were decked with holly, more twinkle lights and occasional surprises, such as the child-size marionette elf that seemed to peer down at shoppers, following their progress through the forest of decorated trees. Subtly hidden diffusers mixed the scent of cinnamon with vanilla and pine, making the aroma of the shop nearly as delicious as the Pruitt home had been the day before. The cheerful murmur of staff members helping customers and the bright ring of the old-fashioned register blended with the dulcet, recorded tones of Gloria Estefan crooning "Silver Bells" to create a cozy atmosphere. To top it all off, just past the stenciled frost on the showcase windows, Roxy could see that it had begun to snow, the flakes looking large, powdery and picturesque.

The single flaw was Nate Carrington standing in the midst of it all.

And he was more appealing than any of her gorgeous displays.

Considering that he was currently in direct competition with her, she hated to admit such a thought had even crossed her mind. But it had. It was also *oh, so true.*

He had abandoned the three-piece suit of yesterday in favor of snug-fitting jeans, sturdy-soled hiking boots and a heavy cable-knit sweater of midnight blue. The sweater hugged his shoulders nearly as closely as the jeans did his hips and thighs. Susceptible women might actually feel the urge to throw themselves against his broad, hard, muscled length.

Until now, Roxy hadn't realized she was that kind of woman.

And as if that wasn't enough, she found she had an almost uncontrollable urge to bury her fingers in the thick waves of Nate's longish, fair hair. Beneath the flickering lights in the rafters the sandy-blond locks looked as rich in color as a casket of Spanish doubloons. The North Wind had already given in to temptation and run her fingers through his hair, tousling it. Roxy wished she could smooth it, then muss it herself, to see if the bright, glowing strands were as soft as angel's hair.

Since Bridget was shadowing his every move, Roxy guessed that Nate was the "hunk" who'd been "browsing," although *browsing* seemed an inaccurate word to describe the way he was studying the merchandise. *Casing the joint*—now that fit what he was doing far better.

Although she was still a distance away, when Nate turned slightly in his contemplation of her Victorian-theme tree, she saw he was making no secret of his identity. The Carrington Christmas Catalog logo was embroidered on his sweater just to the left of where his heart would be.

If he had one.

She was inclined to doubt the organ's existence. Fiends didn't have hearts, and Carrington was surely one of their ilk. How else could he have known to turn up within an hour of Wally and Goldy Pruitt's arrival? Without a doubt, Nate had come solely to make sure they weren't impressed with The North Pole Outlet. That had to be the only reason he was scowling at the fragile ornaments she had so lovingly chosen.

Nate was the only person ever to find fault with this particular tree. It was the most oohed-and-aahed-over display in the whole store, especially with the women shoppers who loved the ribbons, lace, pastel colors and delicate, old-fashioned ornaments.

For the first time since opening her doors to the public, Roxy wished she had a big bruiser of an elf working for her. Some muscle-bound guy who could sweep the floor with Nate before giving him the old heave-ho. In lieu of such an employee, she drew herself up and stormed over to do the job herself.

Nate looked up at her approach, his glance scanning her from head to foot in the kind of masculine appraisal Roxy hated receiving. Rather than be ticked off at getting a quick once-over this time, she found herself wondering if she had passed inspection. His appearance had certainly been above par with hers.

If Nate approved of her winter-white slacks and the sequined snowflake design on her silver angora sweater, he wasn't showing it. Rather than flash the megawatt smile she half expected, Nate deepened his frown. He jerked his thumb toward the tree. "You got these thingamabobs from Paxton and Poindexter Imports, didn't you?''

Roxy skidded to a halt. *Hello. I'm fine. How are you today, Carrington?* she said silently, then went on the defensive. "What if I did?" She wasn't really sure which supplier had shipped the feminine-looking pomanders. She dealt with at least a dozen or more wholesalers and placed orders for more than a single item with each. Only a search of her records would pinpoint from whom she had received these particular ornaments.

"You take one apart to examine the workmanship?" Nate asked.

"They're hand-painted china," Roxy said. "Fine china."

Nate snorted. "Not so fine as the ones we carry at the Triple C."

Naturally he would think so. "Your sales rep showed me the Carrington ones. I liked these better."

Nate looked back at the rival supplier's pomanders and shook his head. "Unbelievable," he murmured. "I'll send you a case of ours free of charge. You can use them as giveaways if you want. A free whatchamacallit with every purchase over fifty dollars."

If he sent them, Roxy decided, she would give the whatchamacallits away, only with a twenty-five dollar purchase. Maybe a ten-dollar one.

Pleased with the idea, she relaxed her guard somewhat and gave him an amused smile. "What are you doing here, Nate? Other than maligning your competitor's merchandise, that is."

"Me?" He turned back to her, this time switching on the full power of his sexy grin.

She should have been prepared for it. She wasn't.

"I've come to take you to lunch," Nate said.

The smile faded from her lips. "No, really," she said, fighting down the flicker of excitement that raced through her at his casual announcement. She couldn't react to him on a purely man-woman level. To do so when they were rivals in a bidding war would be business suicide.

Nate's lazy smile was as lethal as a loaded pistol. "Since when does a man have to have a hidden agenda if he wants to enjoy a beautiful woman's company over a meal?"

Since forever. "Forgive me if I'm mistrustful of you," Roxy said, her voice thick with sarcasm.

His grin didn't dim. If anything, the sparks of mischief in his eyes heightened. He leaned closer, closing the distance between them. They were so close the carefully concocted scent of the shop faded away, replaced by the subtly faint, tangy scent of his aftershave.

"You think I'm here to talk you out of hiring Wally Pruitt, don't you?" Nate said. "The thought never entered my mind."

Yeah. Right. And the next issue of Carrington's Christmas Catalog would feature one heck of a combo deal on the Brooklyn Bridge and oceanfront property in Arizona.

"I appreciate the offer, however—"

"Don't tell me you've already had lunch," Nate insisted. "I know it's nearly two, but it's my experience that retail shop owners have a hard time prying themselves away from their businesses at this time of year. Even if you did grab a bite earlier, you probably could use a break about now."

She could. And she hadn't remembered lunch. That didn't mean she should give in to temptation and accept his invitation. She wasn't hungry—

As if on cue, Roxy's stomach gave a muted growl.

If he heard, Nate was gentlemanly enough to ignore the

sound. "Just a quick bite," he urged. "There's an ice-cream joint that sells sandwiches not two blocks away. The Dairy Deli. We can be in and out in nothing flat."

She shouldn't go. She'd done without a midday meal dozens of times, ignoring the moaning reminders her stomach insisted upon giving her. It wasn't long until Wally and Goldy were due to arrive. Roxy glanced at her watch. If they arrived early, she had maybe forty-five minutes to spare. Not a lot of time when one considered Nate needed to be gotten rid of—if she actually went to lunch with him—before the Pruitts pulled into the parking lot. Prudence argued that she turn him down, that she follow her business instinct and kick him out of her shop. The attraction she felt for him—surely unnatural, considering everything—kept her vacillating over the decision a bit longer. If she procrastinated long enough, there wouldn't be time for lunch and she could send him on his way without feeling she'd made a major mistake.

Boy, were emotions ever hell to cope with!

Inwardly, Nate gloated slightly. He could tell Roxy was seesawing over his invitation. She was right to do so, but he doubted she knew the real reason why. He was a shark when it came to business. If he really wanted Walter Pruitt on his payroll, Walter Pruitt would be on it. But he'd been rethinking things, altering his plan. And all because he hadn't been able to get Roxanne Mercer off his mind since meeting her.

Did she have any idea just how numb his mind went around her? He couldn't have made a coherent business decision, even if the existence of his company depended upon it, with her standing so near. Her hair was upswept today and beginning to fall in delightfully untidy strands at the nape of her neck and around her face. The soft texture of her sweater hugged curves from upper thigh to collarbone; curves he'd only fantasized about—and done a damn good job of guessing at, too!

The shop smelled great but Roxy smelled even better. Not of some musky or flowery scent, but of woman. The hunter in him couldn't resist the scent.

She brushed fretfully at the russet strands flying about her face. She avoided meeting his eyes. "I really can't—" she began when another young woman stepped between them.

The newcomer was a sprite of a brunette a few years younger than Roxy. Although she was wearing a name tag that read Vixen on her red bib apron, Nate doubted that her parents had so christened her. "Did I hear you mention the Dairy Deli?" Vixen asked.

Since Roxy didn't look happy over the interruption, Nate decided to turn on the charm. He stuck out his hand. "Yeah, I did. I'm Nate Carrington."

Vixen shook his hand and nodded at the insignia on his sweater. "Of the catalog of the same name, I assume. Bridget Davenport. Nice to meet you. I really like the merchandise your company carries, Mr. Carrington. I just wish you had a factory showroom where I could buy stuff."

At least someone was wholeheartedly behind Triple C stock. "Ah, come on," he teased. "We're only a couple of miles away from here. We try to ship within twenty-four hours of all phone orders. You probably get your stuff within two days. And the name's Nate."

Bridget responded eagerly, visibly melting beneath his smile. It was nice to know he hadn't entirely lost his touch, even if Roxy was bent on resisting him.

"Well, yeah, I do get my order really fast," Bridget admitted.

Roxy's brow clouded. Probably ticked off that one of her people was so lost to decency as to order holiday decorations elsewhere. It was certainly how he would have felt in her place.

"But think how much more I'd buy if I saw the stuff in person, Nate," Bridget continued. "We do a lot of business in spur-of-the-moment buys here at the Outlet, don't we, Roxy?"

"Yes, but—"

Bridget swept right on with barely a pause, neatly cutting her boss off. "Oh, but you're both off to lunch and I'm holding you up! I didn't mean to butt in, but could you bring me back a sandwich from the Dairy Deli? I've got a craving for a turkey club, and I don't want to leave the shop since we've got a new employee coming in for training this afternoon."

That he knew. In fact, he'd had a hand in making sure Roxy had an opening that needed filling. He also knew that Bridget's request was nothing more than an excuse to make him notice her. He knew for a fact that the Dairy Deli delivered to businesses within a five-mile radius, one that both the Triple C and the Outlet were well within.

"Turkey club," he repeated. "Mustard, mayo? What else do you want? Fries? Cola?"

Roxy, he noted, was doing a slow burn, obviously re-evaluating this particular staff member's performance rating.

"While I get Bridget's order, why don't you grab your coat," he suggested to Roxy. "My car's right outside."

She turned her disapproving look on him. "I don't think that—"

"Did I hear you're getting takeout?" another red-aproned woman asked.

Roxy sighed deeply. The action did great things to the

front of her sweater. He had a hard time keeping his eyes away from the glitter of moving sequins. "I'll be right back," she said and walked away.

She looked almost as good leaving as she did arriving. Nate was so interested in Roxy's retreat, he missed hearing the second staffer's complicated corned-beef order.

3

Knowing she needed her head examined, Roxy back-tracked to her office to gather up her coat and purse. There wasn't time to dawdle so she accomplished the trip in record time. Nate would probably view her rush as eagerness to be with him.

He wouldn't be entirely wrong, either. And not just because she figured her employees would get a lot more work done once he was out of the shop.

If only the situation were different. If only they hadn't met under difficult circumstances.

If only she could regain a modicum of her usual common sense where men were concerned. What was the matter with her? She hadn't thought this much about any man—not even the ones she'd dated more than once—in…in…well, ever! Nate was disrupting her tidy little world, and not just by trying to woo Wally Pruitt into working for Carrington's Christmas Catalog, either.

Although she'd been gone less than three minutes, by the time Roxy returned to Nate's side, she found he had collected sandwich orders from no fewer than four of her employees. Not a one of whom had missed lunch earlier. Knowing the orders were given out of curiosity, not hunger, did nothing for her peace of mind.

Nor did the natural, protective way Nate's arm slipped

around her waist as he led her through the store and out the main door.

Outside, the air was electric, the combination of snow and a slight northerly wind adding to the holiday atmosphere. Roxy welcomed the cold on her cheeks. Perhaps it would cool the heat she felt where Nate's hand pressed lightly against her spine. Even the thickness of her wool coat hadn't insulated her against his touch.

"I'm glad you were railroaded into coming out with me," Nate said.

I hope I am, Roxy thought. "Well, I hadn't eaten yet," she confessed.

He looked gratified by her response. "Good. I don't know about you, but I really hate to eat alone."

She doubted he ever had to do so. There was probably a queue of women taking numbers to accompany him anywhere he chose.

Nate's boots crunched on the salt sprinkled on the pavement. The temperature hadn't dropped to freezing yet, but the weather report that morning had promised that it would—Old Man Winter was blowing into town ahead of his solstitial schedule. It was already cold enough that every breath they exhaled was a visible vapor that trailed away quickly in the chilled air.

"I may be going to lunch with you, but it's got to be Dutch treat," Roxy said.

"Dutch treat," Nate mused. "I wonder what they call having separate tabs in Holland?" He fished in his jeans pocket for his keys and alarm decoder. Ahead of them, something beeped on the low-slung red car and the interior light came on. "I'm not letting you pay for your sandwich, though. If it makes you feel better, I'm writing it off as a business expense. You are one of my valued customers and deserve a perk now and then."

Roxy wondered if she was expected to give "perks" in return. She had a pretty good idea of what one would entail—a softly lighted balsam, a roaring fire in the hearth, a mass of richly covered pillows spilling in sultanic splendor on the floor, smooth jazz on the stereo and perhaps vintage wine in delicate-stemmed Italian crystal. Roxy only wished she dared to "perk" Nate back. The fantasy was awfully tempting.

Although the look in his eyes was warm, perhaps he wasn't set on seducing *her*.

"I'm not backing out on this Santa thing," Roxy said. "I intend to have Walter Pruitt working in my shop before the week is out."

Nate pulled open the passenger-side door. "Perhaps he will be. I don't intend to talk about him this afternoon."

"*You* don't." Roxy slipped into the deep bucket seat and looked up at him.

Nate hooked one arm over the top of the door and bent toward her. Until now, Roxy had only thought Santa's eyes twinkled—and then, just in a tale in a storybook. She'd been wrong.

"Didn't your mother ever tell you it was a bad idea to talk about another man when on a date?" Nate asked.

"We aren't on a date," Roxy insisted stubbornly.

"Sure, we are," he said. Stepping back, he swung the door closed.

If he thought that ended the discussion, Nate Carrington had a lot to learn about Roxanne Mary Theresa Mercer. Rather than wait for him to unlock the driver's-side door, Roxy leaned over and flipped the catch, letting the door swing open slightly just as he reached it. The look of surprise on his handsome face at her action pleased her.

"You said you were writing this off on your income tax as business," Roxy reminded him. "That means this isn't a date. It almost sounds like you're after more business from The North Pole Outlet.''

Nate slipped behind the steering wheel and slammed his door shut. "You're reading too much into a simple luncheon date, Rox."

"Am I?" she asked. "Isn't this really a ploy to make me relax my guard so you can seduce Wally Pruitt into working for you?"

Nate turned the key. The engine hummed to life, purring quietly. "Nope," he said. "I don't want Wally as much as I want something else."

"And what is that?"

Nate glanced over at her. "You, Rox. You."

The sound of the car door slamming rang in Nate's ears. "That is the last time I'm honest with a woman," he said out loud as he watched Roxy flee across the parking lot and back into the cozy shop. He'd tried for a touchdown far too early in this game. He should know better by now. If he wanted to win her heart, a guy had to handle a woman as carefully as he did a football. It took the right touch, the right spin on a phrase, just a hint of control when he tossed out the suggestion, and then the touchdown was made. Preferably in the soft confines of a large bed.

He'd blown the call, though. Hadn't gained enough yardage to make a successful pass.

Still, he had the memory of how her eyes had looked for a moment there—as opaque as a handblown, handpainted, imported ornament. Okay, so he was mixing his metaphors. With Roxy, Christmas ornaments just naturally came to mind. She was as delicately made, as richly colored, and as eye-catching as a sparkling holiday display. So he'd gone for the point and fumbled. He'd also seen puzzlement and passion tumble in the depths of her pretty green eyes. Eyes that reflected intelligence, determination and bullheadedness, as well.

He and Roxy had a lot of the same qualities. At least he chose to see *bullheadedness* as a virtue. Roxy would agree with him. Success in business depended a lot on the stubborn refusal to fail.

It wasn't business he had in mind at the moment. However, since the only way Roxy would probably agree to see him was in a business-related arena, for the time being he would play ball wherever she wished. Sooner or later, the playing field would be that comfy bed. They were both business people, so even in the game of love a bit of negotiating was needed first. He wouldn't make the mistake again of saying something that sounded like "Your place or mine?"

He needed to gain a few yards toward the goalposts. Ava would soon be in place to keep him apace of the plays Roxy planned to make. In the meantime, he would see about winning some favor in her home court.

Nate put the Corvette in gear and headed for the Dairy Deli.

Roxy ignored the speaking looks her staff exchanged as she stormed back into the shop. She wouldn't cater to their curiosity, though. Instead, she slipped out of her coat as she returned to her office. She wouldn't brood over the way Nate had turned the tables on her.

Well, not brood a lot.

Seated once more behind the pile of papers she'd abandoned earlier, Roxy put her elbows on the desk, her chin in her hands...and brooded.

Why had she overreacted and fled from him? Sure, she hadn't been expecting Nate's blunt declaration. Oh, she knew there was an unmistakable attraction between them; she just hadn't expected him to tell her he intended to act on it. The other men she had met via business had seen sex as a by-product of completing a successful job—like a toast, only a lot more personal. That wasn't the way she saw it.

She hadn't run away from any of those men, though. She'd made excuses, hadn't returned calls; but she'd never bolted.

Was it because, in this instance, she wasn't doing business *with* Nate. She was bidding against him, had made no bones about the fact that she intended to win Pruitt in the end. She was going to make sure Nate lost, and yet he'd said he wanted her, so she'd run.

It wasn't a logical reaction, and she prided herself on her logic. Logic told her it was natural for her to be attracted to Nate. He was a handsome man, had a sexy smile and a humor and warmth in his eyes that any woman would find hard to resist. She wasn't just any woman. She was one of his customers, which meant every one of those mind-melting grins of his had probably been tossed in pursuit of larger orders.

So why had he said he wanted her?

And why, despite all the evaluation, did she want him, too?

Probably just an imbalance of hormones. She would make an appointment with her doctor, get the problem adjusted, and never scare herself with a backwash of emotion again. It had been that last she had run from, not Nate per se. He was an attractive brute, and she was a healthy, well-adjusted woman. There was nothing wrong with *thinking* about doing more intimate things with him. Outside of their association as wholesaler and retailer, she would enjoy having a relationship with Nate.

But not on his terms.

Unfortunately, her terms were so far-fetched, there wasn't a man in the whole world who would agree to them.

Was it crazy to want something so much you refused to compromise on it? Having a man who loved her would be great, but she'd seen enough failed relationships among her friends to know love wasn't enough to hold a couple together. It especially wasn't enough for her, Roxy admitted sadly. The one constant in her life had always been work, with the result that her life was built around her business, not—like her married sisters—around another person. She wasn't willing to give up the thing she had worked so hard to build, and she had yet to meet a man who was content to come in second behind the Outlet. Nate would be the same; not content unless he was number one—a place that no man would ever hold with her.

Banishing her dreams of romance back to their private sanctum in her heart, Roxy determinedly turned her attention to Outlet paperwork. Before she knew it, the Pruitts had arrived for their tour.

Later that night when the front bell rang, Nate yanked the door open without first learning the identity of his late-night visitor. "What kept you?" he snapped at the bundled-up figure on the porch.

Ava's voice was more sarcastic than usual. "I love you, too, Carrington," she said and tromped heavily into the house.

"Sorry," Nate mumbled as he closed the door. "I'm edgy. So what happened?"

His executive assistant slipped free of her coat, scarf and badly styled, blue-gray wig, throwing each item in turn onto the sofa before sinking languidly onto it herself.

She took a moment more to fluff up her own carefully dyed blond tresses, mumbling over the hopelessness of the exercise as she peered at the flattened locks in the small mirror of her compact. "You know you're incredibly lucky to have someone as unprincipled as me working for you," Ava said.

"It was an unexpected bonus," Nate agreed and dropped into his worn-but-comfortable armchair. The newspaper was spread haphazardly across the carpet and his shoes had been discarded among the litter, as had various pieces of junk mail. A frozen-dinner container smeared with tomato sauce was put in danger of joining the mess on the floor when Nate swung his stocking feet up next to it on the low coffee table. "Now, once again, what happened?" he demanded.

Ava settled more comfortably on the sofa, kicking off her low-heeled, sensible shoes before curling up among the cushions. For a woman who had stoically blown out every one of the sixty candles he had set ablaze on her birthday cake earlier that year, Ava rarely looked, or acted, like other people her age.

But she certainly looked closer to her sixty years in her current getup. He hadn't even known she owned such understated clothing, much less that she would be willing to be seen wearing it in public.

As if reading his mind, Ava shed the charcoal sweater-vest she'd worn with her Harris-tweed A-line skirt and white oxford-cloth blouse. She still reminded him a bit of his late grandmother, but it was only a surface resemblance. The only creature his trusted assistant had traits in common with was a piranha. A detail-oriented piranha.

"This is going to cost you," Ava warned.

Nothing was free much less cheap, especially where Ava was involved. Nate put off finding out just how costly. "I know. Stop torturing me," he pleaded, then bleated for the third time, "What happened?"

"Remember how you thought making photocopies of all the checks we receive was a waste of time?" Ava asked.

"I take that back," Nate said. "It's a wonderful idea." He paused. "Why was it such a wonderful idea?"

"Because having a copy of one of The North Pole Outlet's checks saved me considerable time," Ava said.

"Oh, in that case..."

Ava ignored his sarcasm. "Roxanne Mercer isn't like you," she explained. "Her accountant is authorized to issue payments to her suppliers, among which the Triple C numbers. You'll never guess whose signature I found on the copies of her checks."

Having been thus warned, Nate knew exactly who the fellow was. "Kenton Clifford McMichael."

"Exactly," Ava purred, pleased for once with his mental capabilities. "Your own accountant."

Not to mention longtime buddy, Nate added silently. As such, he knew Casey McMichael would never give out information on another client, no matter how close a friend was asking the favor. Especially not the kind of information for which he'd sent Ava digging earlier that day. "So, who'd you blackmail in McMichael's office to get the goods on Roxy's payroll?" Nate asked.

"No one." Ava admired the buffed gleam of her fingernails, an action Nate had learned to recognize as her "Damn, I'm good" pose. "When I can't hack my way into a system as unsophisticated as McMichael's, I'll turn in my resignation," she said. "Of course, considering how easy it was to crack, you might consider switching to a more security-conscious accountant."

She meant her nephew. It was an oft-repeated suggestion and one he wasn't about to take.

Nate swung his feet off the coffee table and stood.
"You want some coffee?"

Ava screwed her face up in distaste. "At this hour? I'm
just here to quickly report, then head home so I can enjoy
a well-deserved stiff drink. Do you know the horrors I
have endured for your sake today?"

He didn't, but knew she would tell him in unnecessary
detail anyway. Listening with only half an ear while he
made a fresh pot of coffee, Nate learned the name of
Roxy's newest employee and how much it had cost him
to buy her out of her temporary holiday job—one that
Ava had then stepped in to fill. By the time he poured a
cup and was adding sugar and cream, Ava was regaling
him with her opinion of the antiquated cash register the
Outlet used. He fished a stale doughnut out of the bread
box as she insisted that the red-apron uniform she was
forced to wear made her complexion look ghastly and
swore that if one more person addressed her as
"Prancer," which was what her name tag read, she would
scream.

Funny. He'd roamed Roxy's place for nearly half an
hour that day and he hadn't noticed any of the things that
irritated Ava so. He remembered the tasteful, tempting
arrangement of merchandise, and the fact that Roxy was
carrying far too much stuff from his competitions' ware-
houses.

And how mind-bogglingly beautiful Roxy had been.

Nate wished Ava would mention Roxy. Tell him what
she thought of the Outlet's owner personally. Despite her
somewhat-abrasive personality, he considered Ava family.
He valued her opinion.

Especially when it came to the one woman whose memory truly haunted him.

He had started out the day reliving the time he and Roxy had spent at the Pruitts' home, evaluating it in terms of strategy to get what he wanted. At breakfast, that goal had been to have Pruitt work for him. By the time he'd finished showering and shaving, Pruitt was losing ground. Although he still liked the idea of adding Wally to his own payroll, he was far more interested in adding Roxy Mercer to his life.

It wasn't an admission he could make to anyone else at this point, particularly not to Ava, who had not relished his suggestion that she go undercover at Roxy's shop. She'd only done so because she believed he was genuinely interested in knowing what Roxy was doing to lure Wally into working for her. If Ava knew his priorities had changed, she probably would refuse to continue the masquerade.

He couldn't let that happen. Ava's infiltration at The North Pole Outlet offered the perfect opportunity for him to learn more about Roxy. He definitely needed all the information his assistant could gather, because Roxanne Mercer was the only woman who had ever turned her back and walked away from him. It wasn't a sensation he wished to repeat. Particularly not with Roxy. Besides, although she had certainly tried to look right through him, he wasn't entirely convinced that she was as disinterested as she appeared. He wanted her because she was a beautiful woman. He was intrigued because she'd irked him by storming off rather than have lunch with him. So, from now on, the real reason he went after Pruitt was that doing so gave him an excuse to rub against Roxy.

If only he *could* rub against Roxy. Take her in his arms

and kiss those tempting, ruby lips of hers. Bury his fingers in her russet locks.

"I met Roxanne Mercer briefly," Ava said.

Trying to act nonchalant, Nate settled in his chair once more. "What did you think of her?"

"She seems to be a thoughtful employer," Ava allowed, "but she was more interested in showing the Pruitts around her shop than she was in getting to know her newest employee. They got there practically on my heels."

Nate knew. After delivering the staff's lunch order at the Outlet, he'd driven around the block as a blind, then parked in the lot across the street. He'd slunk low in his seat, feeling like a TV cop on a stakeout, and watched Ava and then the Pruitts arrive. Wally and his wife had looked fairly jolly when Roxy walked them back to their car an hour later.

"And…" he coached Ava.

The look she leveled at him would have made a stevedore think again before interrupting her. "Listen, Carrington, I've been through more than enough today. Don't rush me. You know how much I love dealing with the public—"

She hated it.

"And working past nine in the evening—"

Well, working on something other than her social life, Nate mentally amended, which was far more active than his had been lately.

"So being forced to assist Outlet customers and learn closing procedures once they locked the doors—at nine, if you will!—I'm a little testy," Ava warned.

Only a little? Nate bit his tongue rather than make a comment and kept his attention on the delicate business of dunking his doughnut without slopping coffee on his trousers.

"I like her," Ava confessed quietly, once her ire was spent.

"Humph?" Nate asked, his mouth full of java-drenched cake.

"Roxanne Mercer, that's who," Ava answered, correctly interpreting his question. "Although our meeting was brief, she was very cordial."

"Was she?"

"Pretty, too."

"Is she?"

Nate knew he'd overdone the disinterested tone of voice when Ava gave a ladylike snort of disgust.

"I would have thought you noticed," she said. "You have had a propensity for long-legged beauties in the past."

"Have I really?" He wondered idly who those long-legged beauties had been. The only form that came readily to mind at the moment was the graceful one of Roxy Mercer, and the fire he recalled seeing in her lovely green eyes wasn't one he had found terribly encouraging. Not that it in any way dissuaded him. She was, without a doubt, one of the best-looking women ever to come down the pike as far as he was concerned. Now was not the time to let Ava know he felt that way, though.

Determined to cover his real interest from his assistant's sharp eyes, Nate finished off the last of his dripping doughnut. "So, did you overhear anything Pruitt or his wife might have said about joining the staff during their visit to Roxy's shop? Did she make him a new offer?"

Ava stretched. "No," she said.

"No to which question?"

"Both."

Nate frowned as his assistant gave a deep, heartfelt sigh.

"Give it a rest, Carrington. I may well be your mole in this matter, but Roxanne and her staff see me only as a lowly being hired to do their bidding, not yours. I was kept busy one way or another from the moment I walked in the door until I dropped thankfully behind the wheel of my car, which, I might remind you, was not long ago."

Nate opened his mouth, but Ava forestalled any comment he might make.

"Still, I remember quite well which of you pays me the most, and I did pick up a few tidbits you can chew over to your heart's content," Ava assured. "While the Pruitt couple gushed about this and that during their tour of the place, particularly a bunch of red silk flowers near the register—"

He remembered them well. Roses and poinsettias.

"I never once heard anything that would lead me to believe that Pruitt will be back in the lunchroom sharing takeout with the rest of us very soon. Relax. If you're that worried, give him a look-see at the Triple C for comparison."

Earlier he'd considered doing just that and had rejected the idea. After touring a retail shop where merchandise was not only on display but enhanced through its artistic placement on artificial Christmas trees, walking through a warehouse full of carefully labeled cardboard boxes would be pretty flat. No, while he needed to do something to keep his name on the Pruitts' tongues—if only to keep himself on Roxy's mind—it couldn't be the same thing she had just done. It had to be different. Something shrewd, cunning. Devious. Something she was bound to hear about. But what? Well, he had all night to ponder that question. Right now, it was time to reward the efficiency of his indispensable right hand.

"Good job, Ava," Nate declared. "Why don't you take tomorrow off? You've earned it."

Ava rolled her eyes and felt around for her discarded ugly-but-sensible shoes. "Generous of you, Carrington," she allowed, her voice dripping with sarcasm once more. "But I'm scheduled to work at the Outlet tomorrow."

When she reached for her coat, Nate got up to hold it for her—a service he had performed so often over the years that the self-sufficient Ava had stopped reminding him that she was perfectly capable of donning it on her own.

"You know," she said, "from what I saw and learned of Roxanne Mercer, she reminds me a lot of someone I know."

"Really?" Nate asked. "Who?"

A faint grin curved the corners of his assistant's mouth as she shoved the gray-haired wig in her purse. "You, Carrington," she announced. "You."

A delivery truck from Carrington's Christmas Catalog was waiting outside when Roxy opened the Outlet for business the next morning. There was no note, either of apology or coercion, with the gross of china pomanders, but the packing list was marked "No Charge—Promotional Materials." Nate was right; the quality of his pomanders was superior. They were also the wrong color for her Victorian tree. The man knew how to choose merchandise, he just hadn't a clue about putting together a tempting display.

Roxy unpacked a dozen or so of the fragile china cinnamon-and-citrus-scented pomanders with a Dresden blue portrait of a partridge in a pear tree painted on the side,

and arranged them in a basket to place next to the register.
Then she turned to her PC to print up appropriate signage.
"Say the magic words and win a scented ornament." The
magic words were either "Merry Christmas" or "Happy
Holidays."

Rather than gush over the pretty giveaways as expected,
Bridget looked surprised when Roxy appeared at the register with the basket on her arm.

"You must have just missed my buzz on your inter-
com," Bridget said. "You've got a call on line one."

"Who is it?" Roxy asked, suspicious now that Nate
Carrington had thoroughly seduced her staff with a free,
not to mention unnecessary lunch the day before.

"Mrs. Pruitt," Bridget answered. "Why? You expecting a call from Nate? By the way, what did he say yesterday that sent you storming back in here?"

*Something I'd love to have heard if we weren't in com-
petition,* Roxy thought. "Goldy Pruitt?" she said instead.
"I'd better get that. It might be good news."

Hoping that the call *did* mean she was about to gain
her longed-for Santa, Roxy hurried back to her office.

"Goldy! It's so nice to hear from you this morning,"
she greeted.

"Thank you, dear," Marigold murmured. "Wally and
I just wanted to say how much we appreciated you taking
time to give us a tour of your lovely business yesterday."

While pleasant, they weren't exactly the words Roxy
longed to hear. She clamped down on the disappointment
that threatened to destroy her good mood. With two businesses vying for him, it was probably too much to hope
that Wally had made a decision in under forty-eight hours.

"It was no trouble at all, but a true delight," she assured Goldy. "It isn't often I get a chance to show the
place off."

Marigold chuckled softly. "I quite understand. The Outlet is your life and you have every reason to be proud of it."

Of her shop or of her life? Roxy wondered. While she was button-popping proud of her success, she had to confess that she hadn't been content with either her business or her life for a while now. It was a nebulous discontent, though, and sure to pass. Or so she'd been telling herself for the past year.

"Wally and I have been making do with the decorations we bought our first Christmas together, so neither of us realized there was such a variety of ornament styles today," Goldy continued. "Now that I've discovered them, I'd really like to add a few of the more expensive pieces to our collection."

Roxy hoped Goldy recalled that employees at The North Pole Outlet received a twenty-percent discount on all items in the store. Such an incentive might bode well when Wally made his final decision. "You were rather taken with the reverse-painted ornaments," Roxy said. "They are really beautiful, aren't they?" While the ruddy-cheeked giant had reeled at the price tag on the luxurious creations, his wife had appreciated the beauty and craftsmanship of each opulent piece.

"Oh, yes. I especially liked—" Goldy broke off. "What in the world?"

As Roxy listened, her caller gave a deep, sensual laugh. "The dear boy," Goldy murmured away from the phone. "Yes, by all means, Wally. Put them on the kitchen table. I don't think we've another table large enough to hold them.

"Roxy, do you recall how much I admired the arrangement of artificial poinsettias and roses near your cash register yesterday?" Goldy asked.

"Yes," Roxy said slowly. She had a feeling she wasn't going to like what came next.

"Well," Goldy announced, amusement lingering in her voice, "I just received a very similar-looking arrangement from Nate Carrington, only the flowers are real and the whole thing must be over four feet long and three feet high. I had no idea that florists went in for this scale, did you?"

Roxy not only knew they did, she started planning the scale of the arrangement she would order to cover Nate's coffin after she killed him for executing such a diabolical bit of one-upmanship.

"Oh, Wally!" Goldy called out. "Watch how you maneuver through the doorway. Roxy, dear, I'd best go help him. Again, thank you so much for the tour yesterday. If we don't see you again before the holiday, have a wonderful one."

When the line went dead, Roxy sat grinding her teeth in frustration. Damn Carrington. She'd been fairly sure that Wally would choose her over Nate. Not anymore, though. Goldy was probably on the phone this very minute exclaiming her thanks to the underhanded catalog-owning creep. It only followed that her spouse would favor the Triple C over the Outlet when it came to tugging on his red suit again.

She couldn't let that happen. While her original plan in courting the Pruitts had been to gain a live Santa for her store—especially one who came with built-in, business-generating media coverage—it was no longer foremost in Roxy's mind. She was going to win the war over Pruitt for no other reason than to get the upper hand with that fiendish-minded, devilishly handsome Nate Carrington.

And the first order of business was to dislodge that outrageous flower arrangement from the Pruitts' kitchen table.

Roxy riffled hastily through her phone files, then placed another call.

4

The afternoon sun had begun its descent into the west when Nate met Kenton Clifford McMichael at the high-school stadium. Out on the field the latest crop of teenage athletes buffeted each other in practice, seemingly unaware of the muddy-looking slush on the playing field or of the rapidly dropping temperature. Nate was all too aware that it was getting colder. Turning up the collar of his fleece-lined coat, he wondered if he'd ever been as numb to the cold as the kids on the field seemed to be as they trained for the Friday-night football game—the last of the regular season, which had run later than usual due to a stadium power outage and a string of torrential fall storms.

Nate was glad to see that Casey felt the chill as much as he did. His longtime friend had his chin tucked low into the rolled neckline of the bulky fisherman's sweater he wore under his trench coat. His black hair had been ruffled out of its usual perfection by the wind; but even messed, the premature gray at the accountant's temples gave him a sophisticated, mature, steady look. His appearance was deceptive, for there was no man less inclined to champagne, caviar and the classics than Casey. He was the original burgers-and-beer, Monday-night-football couch potato, and had once cheered loudly for his favorite female mud wrestler when seated at ringside during a friend's bachelor party. A less accountant-acting guy would be hard to find, even if Casey looked the part often enough, especially when he wore his silver-framed glasses.

They weren't in evidence now, although Casey carried his ever-present, work-loaded leather briefcase under his arm. In his hand was a large bag with the words "Dairy Deli" emblazoned on the side.

It wasn't until they'd climbed into the bleachers and made the required "astute" comments on the movements of the young Spartans scrimmaging on the field below them that Casey casually mentioned a bit of news that nearly destroyed Nate's appetite.

Nate had been sitting with his shoulders hunched against the cold, enjoying his steaming, loaded, double-deck burger. Now he stared blankly at his friend, the chilly temperature and the tantalizing aroma of his dinner forgotten. "She what?" he bleated.

"Roxy Mercer sent this Pruitt couple a basket so full of fruit it would keep King Kong noshing contentedly for days, and topped it off with an invitation for them to lunch with her—and me—tomorrow afternoon at The Midas Touch Café," Casey repeated before biting into his own monster sandwich. "I wish you'd pay attention the first time I say things so I wouldn't have to repeat them."

"I did pay attention the first time," Nate insisted. "I just found it hard to believe that a client of yours could be so underhanded."

"*You're* a client of mine," Casey reminded him, his mouth full. "Apparently you started this stupid contest by sending some flowers or something."

"*I* started it? No way," Nate said. *Continued* it—now that was an entirely different kettle of fish. And, in doing so, it looked like he had gotten Roxy's attention much faster than he would have by sending *her* the flowers. Good. In fact, excellent!

Nate finished off his sandwich in celebration.

He did wonder how Roxy had found out about the floral delivery so quickly. He'd planned on calling her later that night and letting the information sort of slip out during their conversation, but this was working out much better than his own plan.

There was just one glitch. When Roxy took the Pruitts to the upscale restaurant, Casey McMichael was going to be sitting next to her, not him.

"What's she want you along for?" Nate asked, determined to fix that particularly nagging detail.

"Other than the fact that I'm handsome, charming, and I handle all her business affairs?" Casey shrugged. "I have been known to order a mean wine."

"'Mean' hardly covers it," Nate remarked, thinking about some of the nasty-tasting vintages his friend had unearthed over the years. "How come you never told me she was one of your clients?"

Casey raised one eyebrow in mock surprise. "For the same reason I've never told her *you* were one of my clients," he said and sank his teeth into his burger again. His gaze returned to the field where the first-string players were busy sacking the second-string players. "Oomph! Did you see that tackle?"

"Really sloppy," Nate agreed, more interested in doing a bit of devious plotting. "Even you could have brought that guy down better."

"Me?" Casey said. "I didn't play football when we were at Adams. That was you. *I* was the star of the basketball team."

"That's what I mean," Nate remarked. "Even a basketball player could have done that play better. However, if you think you were a star player, you've got the world's faultiest memory. As I remember it, you were voted least likely to put the ball through the hoop. Which is why you need to back out on this lunch thing tomorrow.''

''So what if I was?'' Casey demanded. ''What does my reputation back in high school have to do with this business luncheon?''

''It's Roxanne Mercer. You won't be able to keep your mind on business,'' Nate said.

''You don't know Roxy well, do you?'' Casey said.

''Not yet,'' Nate agreed. ''I think you should find a replacement for tomorrow, and I think the replacement should be me.''

''You?''

''You got a problem with that?''

''Yeah, as a matter of fact, I do,'' Casey grumbled, reaching for his foam cup of hot coffee. ''Why do you want to be there? For one thing, you can't fill in for me in a business discussion with one of my clients. For another, this Santa guy is going to be there and you seem to be engaged in some all-out war of acquisition with Roxy.''

''True,'' Nate said. ''She and I only met on Monday, and it was pretty much a case of distrust at first sight—at least on her part.''

''Gee, I wonder why?'' Casey murmured.

Nate ignored the comment. ''That's why I need to be at that table tomorrow.''

''Because you're interested in her?'' Casey asked.

''Now there's a really stupid question, if I ever heard one,'' Nate said. He reached down to retrieve the fast-food sack. ''Did you get any fries?''

''And you think *I* ask stupid questions,'' Casey muttered. "You said burgers and coffee—that's exactly what I got." He paused for a moment to watch prized quarterback Wayne Huffman heave the football to the opposite end of the field where it was snagged by one of the other players. "Roxy is a gorgeous woman, but take it from me, pal, she's got a one-track mind and it ain't on anything a man can supply."

"Yeah?" Nate leaned back, his forearms resting on the stadium bench behind them. "How do you know?"

"I don't know. I'm guessing," Casey confessed. "For all I know, she wants the sun, the moon, and the stars. All she talks about when she's with me is the Outlet, and believe me, I've tried to change the conversation. It doesn't work. You can't derail her. She's all business and nothin' but business."

So was he, Nate mused, but the track he was chugging down wasn't one related to business. Roxy was a beauty, all right. He ought to know since he'd won and lost a good many beautiful women. However, Roxy could have been the plainest creature on earth and it wouldn't have mattered. Fortunately she was gorgeous, but the real reason he was hot to pursue her was because he was irked that she wasn't pursuing him. It was a novel—and ego deflating—experience. And one he was going to turn around even if it killed him.

The last rays of the sun cast long shadows across the playing field below them. The coach's whistle sounded, calling the team in for a final huddle before they broke and headed toward the locker room.

Nate stared after them for a moment. "I need to do this, Case," he said. "I need to be at Roxy's luncheon tomorrow."

"You're nuts," Casey declared.

Nate stretched lazily, then grinned at his friend. "Yeah, guess so."

"I'd have to have a reason for backing out."

"Conflict of interest," Nate offered. "You're my accountant as well as hers. If she wanted you to do some negotiating, you can't do it and be fair to both of us."

Casey didn't look sold on the idea. "And what reason would you give for showing up in my place?"

"That I'm hungry?" Nate suggested.

He waited while Casey mulled things over. "You ever eat at The Midas Touch before?" Casey asked.

"Nope."

"Well, stay away from the curried rice when you order tomorrow. That stuff is hot enough to blow your head off."

Roxy lingered in her office Thursday morning. She was finding it hard to concentrate on the day-to-day chores of running her business. Things on the sales floor ran smoothly, thanks to Bridget's efficiency in managing the other employees. That left the paperwork to Roxy—something she usually enjoyed doing. Except for this morning.

It was only natural for her to be thinking about what she could say to bring Wally Pruitt to the point of making a decision quickly since the holiday season was ticking away. To further convince him that The North Pole Outlet was a thriving business, she had invited Casey McMichael to join them and spout an abbreviated financial report.

Besides, when Casey was along, table-side service always improved. And not because he cut such an impressive figure. He was a big tipper, which was something restaurant staffers remembered and catered to.

Casey could be counted on to keep the conversation business-related, too, which was an area of definite concern when it came to a man and a woman dining together. Other men she had dealt with in regard to the Outlet had seen business as a back door to a cozier relationship. If she'd been the least bit interested in any of them, she would cheerfully have waived her rule of not dating business associates. But she hadn't been interested. Not even a little bit.

Not until she'd met Nate Carrington.

No matter how hard she tried to keep her thoughts centered on winning her in-house Santa, they strayed to Nate. Perhaps it was only a logical progression—Wally to Nate, Nate to...

Well, it was better not to continue that kind of progression.

She had to stop thinking like this. Sales receipts, invoices, packing lists and various bills were threatening to flow out of her In basket and onto the floor. There was work to be done. She had no time for daydreaming.

Yet dream she did.

Of late, she had been loath to return to her empty house each evening, to rooms that seemed to echo despite the comfortable furniture that filled them. She hoped that her mother wasn't right after all and that her growing disenchantment with the status quo was because she had no one with whom to share her success. Although her fond parent had come of age in sync with the women's movement, it didn't mean she'd shed the old-fashioned idea that it took the acquisition of a husband to make a woman's life complete. And after that, a houseful of children.

Roxy prayed that her mother never discovered just how often she found herself wondering if she was right—or even half right. Of course, it only took a few moments of detailing all the responsibilities she had with The North Pole Outlet to whip such sentimental thoughts back to their barred niche in the back of her mind. She had always dreamed of having the freedom of running her own business. There was no reason to relinquish it, even if *freedom* was a far-from-accurate word to describe the reality of that dream.

Still, her mind drifted away from business frequently as it wove a new fantasy for her to dwell on. One in which a strong, loving man greeted her at the end of the day and children with his smile threw themselves happily into her arms.

The dream man and his offspring had acquired shaggy, slightly wavy fair hair and warm gray eyes in the short time since she'd met and faced off with Nate Carrington.

Too bad the fantasy wasn't realistic enough to include more than coloring and that mesmerizing sexy grin of his.

Ever since Nate's appearance in her store on Tuesday, he had intruded on her thoughts. It had been such a con to tell her he wanted her, not Wally. Well, he was a man—what did she expect? The straight, honest truth? *Think again, Roxy. And* not *about Nate Carrington.*

Yet even when she did manage to concentrate, something seemed to happen that would bring him to mind. She'd found that out too well after flipping through a merchandise flyer only to discover it had come from the now unwelcome Carrington warehouse. If she'd followed her natural inclination, she would have put the pamphlet through the shredder simply because he'd tripped up her plans. She hadn't even taken the Pruitts to lunch, yet Nate had already topped her, presenting the couple with box-seat tickets to the local musical-comedy theater. If Goldy hadn't called asking if they could move up the time they'd agreed on for lunch so she could shop for a new evening ensemble, Roxy wouldn't have learned that she'd been upstaged. Oh, she'd expected it, which was why she'd

bought tickets to opening night of *The Nutcracker* ballet.
The tickets would remain in her purse now, the extrava-
gant price she'd paid for them suddenly seeming paltry.
Maybe she would go to the ballet herself—if she could
find someone to invite. Nearly everyone she knew had a
"significant other" with whom they attended events like
The Nutcracker. Perhaps she would just give the damn
tickets away in an advertising ploy. At least then she
could write them off as a business expense.

There was still an hour remaining before she needed to
leave to reach The Midas Touch. She hoped Casey had
gotten the message she'd left with his receptionist about
the change in time. Perhaps she should have asked that
he call her back. No, Casey was dependable. She had
enough to fret about without adding new things to the list.
Instead, she would do something that would give her a
sense of accomplishment, such as getting through the job
of matching invoices to packing slips. She'd started the
chore and stopped it so often, it was dragging on longer
than usual. If she got the job done, she could take the
batch along with her and give it to Casey at lunch so he
could issue checks. She had found it an excellent business
practice to pay her suppliers promptly. Doing so put her
at the head of their list when it came to hearing about
new merchandise or getting quick delivery.

A firm knock on her open door brought the chore to a
halt once more.

Roxy looked up from her paper-laden desk to find a
stranger waiting patiently. The silver-haired woman was
vaguely familiar. She was wearing the red Outlet apron,
which designated her an employee. "Yes?" Roxy asked.

The woman stepped into the room, glancing, as did
most of the other employees upon first entering the cozy,
crowded sanctum of Roxy's office, at the Christmas or-

naments that hung from fishing line on the ceiling. Her gaze moved to the floor-to-ceiling shelves where angels, elves, snowmen and Victorian carolers of cloth, wood and plaster rubbed shoulders with a variety of Santa Claus figures. Garlands of tinsel, roses, holly and poinsettias trimmed an area devoted to creches, menorahs and Steinbach nutcrackers. A small love seat fronted the wide desk. It was upholstered in a green, red and gold print, and piled high with toss pillows that ranged from patchwork to cross-stitch to painted silk, all with holiday designs.

"Eclectic, isn't it?" Roxy said with a grin. She got up and moved around the desk to a more personable distance. "I've kept one of each of my favorite pieces of merchandise over the years. One of these days I'll either hold a manager's-choice sale to get rid of them, or get a bigger office."

"I like it," the woman declared, her voice crisp and decisive. "We met the other day. I'm Ava."

"And I'm Roxy," she said, extending her hand in welcome. "I'm sorry I didn't have time to chat much with you before now. I hope Bridget told you my door is always open if you have a question she can't answer or a suggestion to make on how we can improve things at the Outlet."

Ava's grip was quick and businesslike. "She did, and that last is why I'm here."

Although surprised that someone with barely a day's experience on the sales floor already had a suggestion, Roxy indicated that her visitor should continue.

"You've got strings of craft-cut wooden hearts for $9.95," Ava said.

Roxy remembered them. Strung on rough twine, the nine hearts were painted in alternating shades of red, green and antique yellow.

"Well, I've had a couple of customers who wanted just a single heart," Ava continued. "If you take a couple dozen of the strands, cut them into single ornaments, and price them at $1.95 apiece, you'd not only make seventy-five-percent more in retail on them, I think they'd sell faster."

She was quite right, Roxy thought. Nothing sold faster than a low-priced ornament, and the new retail Ava had suggested was quite modest, even if it did make more money for them.

"Ask Bridget to find out how many strands we've got in stock," Roxy said.

"We already looked. You must have ordered a gross because there are 119 left between the stockroom and the floor," Ava reported efficiently.

Roxy reached back to her adding machine. In following her new employee's suggestion, she would make an additional $900 in profit—more than she would no doubt be paying Ava in part-time salary for the duration of the holiday season.

"Go for it," Roxy said. "Tell Bridget to pull all the strands, even those on the decorated trees. We'll not only turn the hearts into single ornaments, we'll offer a deal. Either $1.95 apiece or three for $5.49. We're ahead either way. Good job, Ava. Sounds like you've got a strong background in retailing."

The silver-haired woman rolled one shoulder. "I dabbled a bit in it in the past," she admitted.

"Any other suggestions?"

"Perhaps later," Ava said. "I'm not familiar with all the merchandise in the shop yet."

If I had more employees like you, Roxy mused as the woman returned to the sales floor, *I'd be a millionaire in no time flat.* A glance at her watch showed she had barely half an hour to finish the invoices before she needed to leave for lunch. Putting her amazement over Ava's astute call on the back burner, Roxy returned to work.

"She loved the idea."

"What merchant wouldn't?" Nate said into the phone receiver. "Hell, if I'd thought of this six months ago, *we* would have sold those damn hearts as separate ornaments instead of in strands. My loss in profit will win you points as employee of the month over there. Any idea yet what Roxy's personal taste runs to?"

"Yes and no. Give me another couple of hours," Ava said.

"Take as long as you like."

"I'd like to get off the damn sales floor and back to my comfortable desk at the Triple C," Ava grouched. "But I don't suppose you'll let me."

"Selfish bastard that I am, no, I won't let you. Not until I've got the ammunition I need," Nate said.

Ava sighed deeply. "Fine. I just wish I knew how all this scheming is going to give you better leverage in hiring Pruitt."

The answer was easy, Nate thought after his assistant rang off. It wasn't going to.

Content that his deviousness would pay off very soon, Nate shrugged his overcoat on over his sport coat, checked the mirrorlike polish of his shoes, and headed out the door en route to The Midas Touch. Roxy was going to be surprised to see him there. There wasn't a chance in hell she would be pleasantly surprised, though. At least in a public restaurant she wouldn't try to strangle him.

She'd just look like she wanted to.

Roxy waited patiently by the maître d's podium at The Midas Touch for the Pruitts and Casey to arrive. She'd dressed carefully for this luncheon, choosing a long, pleated, red-and-green tartan skirt and matching vest, a creamy silk blouse with antique-lace trim around the high Victorian collar, and a black velveteen jacket. Hopefully the outfit married her kindred interests of the holidays and business. She wanted to look professional, but relaxed.

Which she wasn't. She was on pins and needles, glancing frequently at her watch. She'd changed their reservation to eleven-thirty at Goldy's request, and it was now after that and she was the only one who'd arrived on time. Did that bode well for a working relationship with Wally? Was he one of those chronically late employees?

She was probably worrying herself into a state for nothing. The streets were a mess, what with the snow of the other day melting a bit, then freezing up overnight. It was snowing again today, but in hard, sleetlike pellets rather than pretty, powdery flakes. The Pruitts were probably tied up in traffic. And Casey? For all she knew, he'd never gotten her message. Well, even if he came in as they were having dessert, he could still say his piece. The idea was to have a pleasant, relaxed meal.

The atmosphere at The Midas Touch Café was tasteful, elegant, and if the prices on the menu matched the decor, pricey. It was the kind of place that catered to those who were successful—or looked successful. The Pruitts should be impressed, and once they were replete with good food and basking in the glow of muted light, she would press Wally to make a decision. The Christmas season was galloping by. If she wasn't going to have her own Santa, she had to know now so other plans could be made.

To keep from fidgeting in impatience, Roxy decided to do what she did best—evaluate the holiday decorations around her.

The front door of the restaurant had a large wreath of gold-sprayed branches entwined with golden ribbon and glitter-dusted gilt ornaments. It looked like a piece straight out of the King Midas legend, a wreath turned to gold at his touch. However, just inside the door the theme hadn't carried over as well. There was a seven-foot-tall blue spruce to the left of the maître d's stand. To do justice to the high ceilings, they needed a taller tree—a short-needled pine, Roxy decided. Rather than be entirely gold, the tree should remain natural. Color was the key. They needed a tree with deeper, lusher green needles to complement the restaurant's decor.

The tree they had needed more ornaments to give it a richer, more opulent texture. While she agreed that gold was the right choice for the decorations, the ornaments should have been varied in design and shape rather than all be identical. And some of the lights should have been twinkle ones to add some excitement and movement. The angel at the top was too traditional and...

Hmm. Instead of mentally redecorating this particular tree, perhaps she should be talking to the restaurant's owners about completely redoing their holiday decor next year. A decorating service was a natural extension of her present business. Customers were always asking—jokingly, she'd thought—if she could send someone over to do their tree. Perhaps they'd been serious. And if they hadn't, she could make them serious by offering exactly that type of service.

She'd trained Bridget, who'd trained the other staff members, in ways to make the most of available ornaments and trim. The trees in her shop were incredibly lovely and quite diversified. With a specially trained very seasonal staff, she could expand the Outlet's scope. It was certainly worth looking into. She would make a note to talk to Casey about it, work on a prospectus, find the time now to identify clients who would benefit from her expertise.

She was just about to pull a notepad from her purse when the street door opened and three people entered, bringing with them a gust of icy, snowflaked wind.

As Goldy and Wally shook off their damp head coverings, the maître d' materialized from the restaurant proper. "Would this be the rest of your party, Ms. Mercer?" he asked in a quiet, refined voice. Roxy wasn't sure, but she felt as if he was less than pleased with her guests. She had chosen The Midas Touch to impress—and treat— the Pruitts. She hadn't thought about how out-of-place the jolly giant and his Junoesque bride would look in the restaurant. Or that they would receive less-than-excellent service. Now she wondered at the appropriateness of her choice.

And there was another problem, as well.

"Yes," Roxy told the maître d'. "And no." She stared straight at the third of the recent arrivals. "What are you doing here?" she asked Nate Carrington.

He flashed her a grin a satyr would kill for. "Filling in for Casey. He couldn't make it. Delighted to be here, too, I might add. And how are you, Rox?"

Nate helped Goldy with her faux-fur-trimmed anorak, then took Wally's scarlet parka from him. "I'll just check these and catch up with you," he said.

"Such a dear boy," Goldy murmured. "So thoughtful. He insisted upon coming to the house to collect us. Not that we mind driving in the snow, of course..."

Wally laid a finger aside of his nose and winked. "The reindeer know the way to carry our sleigh, you see," he said.

Even decked out in a cheap brown wool suit, Pruitt

looked like Santa Claus, Roxy thought. She just *had* to have him in her store.

"Don't tease, dear," Goldy said, but there was a twinkle in her eyes that told Roxy the woman would have loved arriving for lunch in a sleigh drawn by eight tiny reindeer.

Considering Wally's girth and that of his missus, perhaps eight iron-pumping reindeer.

"Nate picked you up?" Roxy echoed, hoping she'd heard wrong. "He drives a two-seater Corvette."

"Not today," Nate said, joining them. He looked the success he was in a well-cut gray tweed sport coat, black turtleneck and black flannel trousers. You could cut a steak with the knife-edge crease of his trousers. Or so Roxy fancied. His hair, however, still needed a trim—badly—although the ragged look was beginning to grow on her. Probably the result of the daydream where she ran her fingers through the sandy-colored mop, grabbing hold to lightly tug him down to where their—

Roxy kicked herself mentally. This was her business luncheon and Carrington had oozed his unwanted way into it. She should be plotting ways to take him out of the Pruitt competition—not fantasizing about being alone with him, about being in his arms.

"I traded cars with Casey," Nate continued. "It may look like the rolling office of a mobster kingpin, but McMichael's black sedan is a smooth-riding vehicle."

At his direction, the Pruitts followed the maître d' across the empty restaurant to a tiny table near the kitchen door. Roxy was about to do the same when Nate took her elbow and held her back. "Did you tip this dude yet?" he asked quietly.

Roxy stared blankly up at Nate. "Tip him?"

"I thought not," Nate said, stopping by a larger table

in the center of the room. He shoved one hand into his pocket and caught the head man's eye. "Wasn't this the table Ms. Mercer reserved?" he asked, the tone of his voice firm and uncompromising.

"But of course. My mistake," the maître d' agreed, having noticed—as Roxy now had—that Nate was holding a folded bit of paper printed with official federal green ink.

A moment later they were all seated at the new table and the man was pocketing whatever denomination of bill Nate had slipped him. Despite herself, Roxy was glad Nate had come to her rescue, even if she hadn't really needed rescuing. She could have paid to get a better table herself—if she'd realized such a thing was needed. She really didn't get out enough to know the restaurateur's code.

Of course, if Casey had shown, *he* would have covered her faux pas. It was one of the things she paid him to do.

Did that mean she was now in Nate's debt? She glanced over at him as he perused the menu a suddenly very attentive waiter had presented. Perhaps it wouldn't be *too* much of an imposition to thank him—not too profusely, naturally.

Just beyond Nate, Roxy had a clear view of the unacceptable Christmas tree in the foyer. She definitely needed to branch out into holiday decorating for private business, if not for private homes. If she created complete trees or themes for trees using merchandise from Carrington's Christmas Catalog, the additional profit from new sales should be a very welcome way of thanking him. He could even incorporate prepackaged tree ensembles among his catalog selections—crediting her with the choice, of course.

She had a feeling that Nate would prefer something a

little more personal, though. When he looked up and caught her studying him, his smile widened wickedly.

The hell with giving him more business. A simple thank-you and a reimbursement for the cash he'd laid out were more than sufficient.

Or so her mind reasoned. Her traitorous libido turned up the heat, sending her blood rushing loudly through her veins in response to Nate's grin.

If things continued in this vein, lunch—no matter how hard the chef worked—was going to be incredibly tasteless. Food paled when compared to the delights her mind preferred to dwell upon.

All because of that damn interfering—enticing—Carrington.

5

Goldy Pruitt waved a final farewell before closing the door. There was a wide, satisfied smile on her face as she listened to Nate drive off.

"Wasn't that a particularly lovely lunch?" she asked, pulling off her knit gloves and shoving them into the pocket of her white anorak.

Wally finished hanging his red parka in the closet and helped her off with her coat. "It was nice, but I would have preferred a bowl of chili and a burger over that bit of prairie chicken I had," he said.

"It wasn't prairie chicken."

"Well, it was a scrawny chicken," Wally insisted, putting her coat away.

"It was guinea hen braised in cream, and very expensive," Goldy said.

"I know. I saw the prices on the menu. Chili still would have been better."

Goldy kissed his cheek. "I wasn't referring to the food anyway, dear, but if it will make you happy, I'll fix chili for dinner."

Wally gave her a fond squeeze. "Bless you. Mind if I take one of those long winter naps until supper? That cream sauce is still sitting right here." He tapped his fist against what had once—long, long ago—been a washboard stomach. Time and Goldy's cooking had taken their toll on it but Wally had no regrets.

"Don't you want to know *why* I think it was a nice luncheon?" Goldy asked, her head cocked to one side.

"Because you had the lamb chops?" he essayed cautiously.

"No. It's because the magic is beginning to work between Nate and Roxanne."

"Oh," Wally said. "That."

"You haven't the least idea what I'm talking about, do you? The combination of Christmas and romance," Goldy said, her tone revealing her irritation over his denseness. "I would have thought you could remember what it was like. *We* fell in love one Christmas."

Wally slipped his arms around her, hoping to lull her back into a chili-making mood. "I fall in love with you all over again every Christmas."

"Not every day?"

"At least three times a day," he assured her.

"I should have known it would have something to do with mealtimes," Goldy said, smiling ruefully. "You're pushing your luck, bub. Besides, how could you not see the magic at work? Nate barely took his eyes off Roxanne, and she was working awfully hard not to look at him."

Wally sighed. "Are you sure about this? Seems to me they squabble a lot for a couple busy falling in love."

"They only bickered over the check and I completely understand that. Roxanne was the one who invited us, so there was no reason why Nate should have tried to pay the tab. She's a successful woman, his equal. She should be treated as such. She's also quite determined not to give in to the magic and fall in love with him," Goldy declared. "We'll probably have to give her a push in the right direction."

"We will, will we?" Wally said skeptically. "How?"

"I haven't decided yet," Goldy said and put a hand gently on her abdomen. "I'll think of something. Right now I need an antacid. That lamb chop didn't like me in the least."

On Friday, things at The North Pole Outlet resembled a beehive with customers coming and going at a honey-high gathering pace. Very few of the stressed-out shoppers issued cheerful holiday greetings, so Roxy changed the catchphrases on the giveaway ornaments to "cash" and "charge," and got rid of Nate's freebie pomanders in record time. To spell her harried, helpful employees, Roxy took over duties at the cash register. Although she personally chose all the merchandise in her store, her staff knew where the various items could be found in the shop and thus were better equipped to help customers. The only elf not on the sales floor was the new hire, Ava. Although fast learning where things were, the older woman wasn't used to standing for long hours at a time. At Bridget's suggestion, Ava was perched on a stool to Roxy's right where she could wrap each of the fragile ornaments in a cushion of tissue paper after Roxy rang them up. The new assignment allowed Ava to rest her aching legs and feet.

Despite the steady stream of customers, when the phone rang, Ava efficiently swooped it up and tucked it between her ear and raised shoulder without breaking stride on the ornament she was wrapping. "Happy holidays! Carr—" She broke off and cleared her throat before continuing. "North Pole Outlet. Can I help you? Yes. Can I tell her who's calling? Just a moment." Another quick, automatic move and Ava had put the caller on hold. "Marigold Pruitt for you, Roxy."

If Goldy was calling to tell her Wally had decided to

go with Carrington's Christmas Catalog, she was going to spit, Roxy decided as she took a charge card from her current customer. "Be right with her. What was that you almost said when you answered?"

Ava shrugged and kept wrapping. "Old habits die hard," she said. "Just the name of another place I've worked."

Roxy laughed softly. "I know what you mean. I've actually answered my phone at home by saying 'North Pole Outlet.'" She handed a charge slip to the customer, indicating where the woman should sign it. "So what did you almost say, Ava?"

"Carter, Claridge and Clifton," Ava answered, her attention more on reaching beneath the counter for a fresh stack of precut tissue paper. "You'd better take your call."

"Carter, Claridge and Clifton," Roxy mused. "Sounds like it was a law firm." She lifted the phone receiver and tucked it under her ear much as Ava had done earlier. Then she took a basket of merchandise from the next customer in line and continued ringing sales as she chatted briefly with Goldy.

It was nearly an hour later, after she'd accepted an invitation to dinner Sunday evening at the Pruitts' and one of the staff elves relieved her for a short break, that Ava's slip of the tongue returned to nag at Roxy.

Carter, Claridge and Clifton. She didn't remember the name appearing on the list of previous employers Ava had supplied on her application. Of course, the employment application only required that the names of employers from the last five years be noted, and Ava's time at Carter, Claridge and Clifton could have predated the limited time span.

But how many people continued to answer the phone

with a former employer's name five years after leaving the firm?

Curious about her newest elf's background, Roxy pulled Ava's file. Sure enough, Carter, Claridge and Clifton wasn't mentioned. The names of recent employers that were noted looked vaguely familiar, though. None of the three had been called before hiring Ava since Roxy trusted Bridget's instinct about the people she employed. But for a woman as efficient and retail savvy as Ava had already shown herself to be, it was strange that not one of her previous jobs had been in retailing.

Roxy picked up the phone.

"It wasn't my idea," Casey McMichael bleated defensively in greeting when his receptionist put Roxy through. "My being at The Midas Touch could have been construed as a conflict of interest on my part because—"

"Relax, Casey," Roxy soothed. "If you've known Nate forever, like he said, he probably threatened to break your arm."

"Close enough," Casey admitted. "So you aren't taking your business to another accountant because I let him take my place at lunch yesterday?"

"Not yet, at any rate," Roxy said, leaving the possibility open, should he not cooperate with her in the future. The very immediate future. "What can you tell me about Fifth Floor Films, Regional Republic and Krosscut Limited?"

"Other than that they are all clients of mine?" Casey asked.

Now she remembered where she'd seen those names. On Casey's promotional-services brochure. And they'd appeared in the same order Ava had written them.

"I'm the only thing they have in common that I know of," Casey continued. "One is a small documentary production company, another is an insurance firm and the third is just a guy who services vending machines and wanted a jazzier company name. Why?''

Roxy drummed her fingers lightly against her desk pad and frowned. She was no longer curious. She was downright suspicious. "One more question, Casey, and it's the $64,000 one.''

She heard Casey swallow loudly before answering.

It was difficult finding a parking space at the strip mall, especially one likely to keep the paint job on his car nick-free, but Nate managed. He was a bit surprised at all the activity. Yeah, it was the holiday season, and, yeah, shopping was a necessary chore if there were to be packages under the tree, but he was still amazed at the hustle and bustle he found just inside the main door at Roxy's place. Granted, his own business didn't maintain a steady pace year-round. It was only from around the middle of August to mid-December that the Triple C was a madhouse with phones steadily ringing, forklifts shifting cases of merchandise, packers filling orders for shipment and trucks pulling in and out of the docking bays. Next to The North Pole Outlet, the action at the Triple C was as tame as sesquicentenarian shuffleboard.

Patrons at the Outlet register were five deep. The level of cheerful chatter pretty well drowned out the recorded background music, although Nate felt Kenny G was blowing his Gabriel best in an effort to be heard. There were at least eight red-aproned staff members flitting about, interacting with customers, their bright smiles looking uniquely sincere despite the press of desperate shoppers. And the axis of it all—or so it seemed to him—was Roxy.

She was radiant, lovely, gorgeous. She, like her workers, wore the Outlet apron today, but on her the berry-red color glowed even brighter. The other times he'd seen her she had been dressed office-smart in a suit or coordinated ensemble. Today she had on a green turtleneck sweater, jeans and soft, ankle-high boots. Her glorious russet hair was pulled back from her face with a clip, yet it brushed her shoulders every time she turned her head. While holiday greetings were issued to every customer, it was the laughing quality of Roxy's voice that seduced one and all.

Particularly him.

Nate queued up with the rest of the customers at the register, patiently awaiting his turn.

She spotted him almost immediately. "Nate! What are you doing here?"

"I've come to make amends," he said loudly, hoping she heard him over the shoppers' buying frenzy. "See?" He lifted the cellophane-wrapped grouping of two-dozen bloodred carnations over the head of the customer in front of him so Roxy could see them as she continued to ring sales.

The customer looked at the flowers skeptically. "The color is right, but roses would have been better," she advised.

"And candy," another woman said as she joined the line behind him. "Didn't you bring her chocolate?"

"I don't know her well enough yet to give her candy," Nate said.

"Trust me, buddy," a man two customers up line from Nate declared as he balanced the packages his wife had piled in his arms. "Without chocolate in hand, you haven't got a chance in hell of ever getting to know her any better than you do now."

As if by magic, Bridget materialized at Nate's elbow. "Whoa. Looks like someone's trying to buy his way out of the doghouse," she said and pulled him out of line. "I can take over for Roxy for about ten minutes, but that's all the time I can give you. It's Christmas, you know.''

The people waiting to pay for their purchases all turned and smiled at him; a few even wished him a happy holiday. The helpful man mouthed the word *chocolate* at him and winked broadly. Then Roxy was at his side, laughing up at him, smiling. Looking happy to see him! Nate forgot exactly why he'd come to her shop. He just knew that if he didn't manage to sweep her into his arms and kiss her breathless soon, he would go mad.

''You didn't need to bring me flowers,'' Roxy said as she led him out of the crush and down a narrow passageway to her storage closet of an office.

Ava hadn't been kidding when she'd told him the place was packed to the rafters. Nate had to duck his head to avoid being brained by some of the ornaments that dangled like stalactites from the ceiling.

He handed over the carnations. ''I don't suppose you have a vase in here anywhere?'' he asked, glancing around.

The pieces she'd chosen to decorate her office told him a lot about Roxy. He liked her taste, and why not? He recognized a number of items that had come from the pages of his own catalog. The fact that she put like items together told him there was a systematic organization in what might look like chaotic clutter to the uninitiated eye. He already liked the layout of her store, and the volume of business he'd just seen was impressive to a man used to dealing with P&L sheets. Yet it was the glow in her pretty eyes, the soft blush on her cheek that held him in thrall. Telltale signs that she was pleased to see him? *In your dreams, Carrington.*

Roxy delighted him by burying her pert little nose among the dark garnet carnation petals. ''No, I'm afraid vases aren't one of my normal stock items. While it isn't aesthetically appealing, I believe there's an empty five-pound coffee can in the break room that will do nicely in the meantime. Thank you for bringing them. They're lovely."

Something more than words would have been appreciated, but Nate remembered the advice given by the unknown man. If he wanted kisses, he should have brought chocolate.

He would next time.

Roxy set the carnations aside on her desk and leaned back against the broad, paper-littered surface. "Now tell me what you've really come here for, Nate," she said.

He took a spot next to her, sitting casually on a batch of invoices. "Must I always have ulterior motives to see you, Rox?"

Her green eyes danced with light. "Yes, Nate," she murmured, amused, "I think you must. So what is it this time?"

Nate took the plunge. "Just to see you. Really. I want to start over. To erase the past and begin fresh."

"We only met a few days ago," Roxy reminded. "I hardly think that constitutes a past."

"Maybe I want one with you," he said. "Or at least a chance at a future, and the more immediate the better."

Because he was finding it difficult to sit so near her and not make a push to bring his fantasies to life, Nate moved away from the desk and roamed over to investigate the nearest shelf unit. The crown of his head brushed against one of the dangling ornaments. He reached up and caught it, stopping it in mid-momentum before it could bump into its nearest neighbor.

The ornament was over three inches in diameter and painted to resemble a star-spangled dark winter sky. The constellation of Taurus was picked out in slightly brighter pinpoints. They'd been available in all twelve astrological signs.

"This one sell well in the store?" Nate asked.

It had sold fairly well through his catalog, but the retail on the lovely imported item had kept it from being a real door buster of a seller.

"Surprisingly, yes," Roxy answered. "I ran out of them."

He wished *he* had. "If you still need some, I think I've got a couple of cases yet."

Roxy looked surprised. "I didn't see them featured in any of the Carrington wholesale flyers. If I had, I would have taken at least six dozen this year."

Six dozen? That was seventy-two ornaments that, if he remembered correctly, retailed for $24.95 each—or better.

"There weren't enough left to merit inclusion in the regular catalog, which was something we didn't realize until after the deadline on the clearance catalog," he said and studied the ornament once more.

Was he making the least bit of headway with Roxy? he wondered. There were a lot of guys who would think he had lost his mind. Here he was, alone with an extremely attractive woman, one he admittedly had the hots for, and he was talking business. But with Roxy, he was pretty sure doing so was the most direct route to her bed.

And besides, he was curious about her business. It was so like his and yet so different.

He indicated the sparkling midnight-blue ornament again. "The price didn't deter shoppers?"

"No, and the Outlet didn't carry that ornament at the suggested list price either," Roxy answered. "We marked it higher."

Higher! His profit-conscious self gave the romantic in

him a shove out of the way that would have been much admired by the members of the current Adams High football team.

"We decided the quality and uniqueness of the piece would sell well at $29.95," Roxy continued. "And we were right. The constellation ball flew out of here. I only wish some of the other higher-priced merchandise did as well."

Thoughts of seduction temporarily shelved, Nate pondered the ramifications of Roxy's claim. "Customers unwilling to pay that kind of price on a lot of stuff, huh?" He had odds and ends like that himself. Really beautiful, expensive pieces that sat gathering dust.

"Unwilling, no," Roxy said. "Usually they want more than a single piece and the cost is simply prohibitive. So, no, I wouldn't say they are unwilling to pay the price as *unable* to do it for more than a single ornament in one fell swoop."

"Why not make the swoop possible?" Nate suggested. He let the ornament spin slightly on the fishing line to which it was attached.

Roxy leaned toward him slightly, appearing interested in what he had to say. "How?" she asked.

Nate was still working on the idea and needed to buy time. "You ever have sales on items of this class?"

She nodded. "They're on sale now for twenty-percent off."

"Good idea. On sale it's practically at the manufacturer's suggested retail."

Roxy grinned. "A little lower. By around ninety-nine cents. The other time of year we run a sale is during our Christmas-in-July event."

Nate did some fast mental math, something he'd become extremely adept at his first year in business. "What about an ornament-a-month club? The deal would be that the customer signs up to get twelve of the better ornaments, two of which they buy on sale, and one that they receive free after they've bought eleven.''

He could tell Roxy was intrigued with the idea. Her eyes narrowed slightly in thought—doing her own mental math, he guessed. He wished she wouldn't chew on the lush fullness of her bottom lip as she thought, though. It made his own brain go fuzzy just when it needed to be sharp and in focus.

''Not a bad idea,'' she allowed. ''But there are still a lot of shoppers who like the exquisite pieces and wouldn't be able to afford that many.''

Had the ancients created a god or goddess of devious minds? Nate wondered. If so, he needed to make an offering at the deity's shrine, because possessing one of the most devious of minds around had just gotten him in like Flynn with Roxy. Nate launched his second hastily concocted marketing ploy.

''Layaway,'' he said. ''It doesn't matter how many ornaments they buy as long as they put down twenty-five percent and pay a small storage charge. All layaway items must be claimed by the end of the calendar year or be returned to stock.''

She wasn't as taken with this suggestion. Roxy frowned a bit. ''So we have odds and ends of merchandise dumped back on the floor just as we gear up for inventory? We have stock tied up for who knows how long and make nothing for the problems that causes?''

''Don't act as if a thousand customers are going to ram the majority of your inventory in layaway,'' Nate recommended. ''It will be a small percentage, and even a smaller percentage of those folks will renege. State up front that there is a restocking charge on unclaimed items.

If Casey tells you that's illegal or something, make the service charge nonrefundable and hefty enough to compensate for the time, space and pain in the bu—''

"I get the idea," Roxy said dryly.

She liked his suggestions, though. He could tell by the mulling-it-all-over expression on her face.

"I like your shop, you know," Nate said. "It's classy, cozy, and stuffed to the gills. Of course, it's got far too much stuff from suppliers other than the Triple C."

The smile in Roxy's eyes had them dancing as warmly as if candles glowed deep in their green depths. When she laughed the sound of her laughter, was quite delightful, falling on his ears with the clarity of Christmas bells on a clear, starlit wintry night.

Maybe he'd just been staring at this particular ornament for too long, Nate thought, giving it a slight twirl before ducking his head to safely retrace his steps back to her desk.

"I knew you'd work in a plug for your catalog somewhere along the way," Roxy said. "Thank you for the suggestions, though. Do they come with a price tag?"

"Dinner?" Nate asked.

She grinned—in amusement rather than acceptance, unfortunately.

"Movie?"

"Nate, it's my busiest time of year."

Well, she hadn't given him an out-and-out no this time. "A drink to unwind," he countered.

"I—"

A tentative-sounding knock on the open door interrupted her.

"Sorry, Roxy," a red-aproned woman said apologetically. "Bridget asked me to ask Mr. Carrington if he can spare you for the rest of the day so she can get off the register.''

Roxy pushed away from the desk. "He's just leaving, aren't you, Nate?''

He guessed he was.

"How about if I give you a call early next week?'' Nate suggested. "Maybe the pace will have eased up long enough for you to swing by for a tour of the Triple C.''

"Maybe,'' Roxy said as she walked with him to the door of her office.

She was giving him the brush-off. Or trying to.

They were in the doorway. In thirty seconds she would have him back in his car, out in the cold, nursing an ego that was shriveling like the vegetables he'd forgotten were in the refrigerator crisper. He might as well return home and commune with them.

"Oh, look,'' the Outlet staffer cried happily. "You're both under the mistletoe.''

Nate glanced up. Sure enough, there was a sprig of green leaves with white berries tied with a scrap of red ribbon stuck almost directly above his head. His spirits perked up.

"Mistletoe!'' Roxy exclaimed, obviously not as thrilled as he was. "Where did that come from?''

"A mistletoe bush?'' her employee offered. "You're stalling, Roxy. You're under it, he's under it. You've got to kiss him.''

"Yeah,'' Nate said, slipping his arms around her. "You have to kiss me. It's the law.''

The red-aproned woman chuckled. "You heard him.''

Roxy sighed. "The law, hmm?'' She slipped her arms around his neck. Looked into his eyes. Rose up on her toes to plant a quick, sexless one on him.

Nate dipped his head to hers. Their lips brushed together lightly, lingered…and then lingered some more.

Sirens went off in Nate's head. Really loud, joyous-sounding ones.

They scared the hell out of him.

Still, Roxy was the first to break away, to end what could easily have become the world's greatest kiss. Her hands continued to rest on his shoulders. "Merry Christmas, Nate," she said, her voice soft and incredibly sexy to his ears.

"Merry Christmas, Roxanne," Nate murmured, wondering if the mistletoe law allowed more than a single smacker. A minimum of two kisses worked well for him—the maximum, even better.

"Do you really have a couple dozen constellation ornaments you can send over?" Roxy asked.

Her voice hadn't returned to its normal pitch. Did the low, almost throaty sound of it mean she had been as affected as he by the all-too-brief kiss?

"I'll bring them back myself," Nate promised, eager for any reason to see her again and possibly lure her back beneath the mistletoe.

Roxy leaned weakly in the doorway watching Nate stride quickly down the narrow hall away from her. How could he have the strength, much less the equilibrium, to do so after that kiss? It hadn't been long, it hadn't been hot, or wet, or passionate. It had been tender, tentative, and mind-numbingly wonderful.

Get yourself together, Roxanne! she silently lectured herself. To no avail. Her legs remained rubbery, her knees ineffectual, and her brain—well, she'd lost it. Not a doubt about that. A sane woman would not be staring like an idiot after a man. A successful woman—which, Roxy reminded herself strongly, she was—would not be so caught up in a hormonal high that she ignored her business. But here she was, doing both the staring and the ignoring.

When Nate turned to flash a brief, promising smile at her before vanishing into the shop, Roxy knew her day was shot as far as regular business was concerned. Ringing sales was a job she could do while brain-dead. However, if she returned to the register she would chat automatically with customers, hit the right keys, give the right change, and all the while she would be thinking of Nate Carrington—of how good it was to have her arms around his neck, of how lovely it was to have his arms around her waist, of how wonderful he smelled, felt and tasted. And of how absolutely awesome that kiss had been.

She'd stared deeply into his long-lashed gray eyes in wonder. Had seen glints of light in them like the reflection of flickering tree lights, or like the stars painted on the opulent ornaments with which he would be returning at her request.

She couldn't face him. Not yet. She needed to sort out, in what remained of her mind, what she wanted or didn't want from Nate, particularly now that she'd coerced Casey into spilling the beans about Nate. The only thing she was sure of was that she wanted the ornaments. Not exactly a life-changing decision, that. Conducting business was so ingrained, she could talk it while unconscious. Which she most definitely had been, to even mention the ornaments while still in the circle of Nate's arms.

The inclination to close her door to the activity in the shop, curl up on the miniature couch and dream about Nate was too strong. She couldn't let herself do it. But she also couldn't carry on business as usual, knowing that he would be returning with the ornaments. And he would be returning that day, probably within the hour.

There was only one cure. Rather than return to the sales floor immediately, Roxy picked up the phone. "Casey, have you got time to see me today? I've got an idea about expanding the Outlet's services and need to discuss it with you." Ten minutes later Roxy was out of the shop and flying—fleeing, she admitted—from her next encounter with Nate Carrington.

Unfortunately, thoughts of him were not as easy to escape.

6

---◆---

The newspaper carried very distressing news Saturday morning. Famine, wars, inflation, crime, and even more shocking than all the rest, a photograph of Walter Pruitt in his Santa suit visiting children at a local hospital ward, the caption stating that he had played the part free of charge.

Roxy grabbed a second, even stronger cup of coffee upon reading the astonishing account. She believed in charity, contributing regularly to various organizations, donating canned goods to the community food bank and apparel and blankets to the homeless shelter. It was all done quietly and anonymously. Wally's act, while gracious and kind and quite in keeping with the season, smacked of advertising his availability.

Did that mean she'd been invited to dinner at the Pruitts the next evening to be given bad news for dessert?

Although she'd been religiously keeping her mind from thinking about Nate—well, almost managing to do so—this was not a time to avoid him and their animal attraction for each other. At least, she thought it was nothing more than animal attraction; pheromones gone wild. She needed to learn what Nate knew with regard to Wally. Besides, after her discussion with Casey the day before, she had spent the evening putting together a holiday decorating-service proposal. To launch it, and garner references for the next season, she'd immediately contacted The Midas Touch Café and volunteered to redo their tree at no cost. If they liked the decadent richness of her creation, they could purchase the decorations at a discount if they signed a contract with her for the following year. Roxy planned to bring in a professional photographer to document her work with before-and-after pictures. But, if she was going to make good on her promise to improve the restaurant's seasonal decor, she needed additional merchandise. And the items she had in mind were all things that needed to be acquired through Carrington's Christmas Catalog. Nate's warehouse was only a couple of miles away, after all.

And as he had invited her to come for a tour, she had more than enough reason to take him up on the offer. There was The Midas Touch job, and Wally's subtle ad, as well as her curiosity as a Carrington client to see the setup at the Triple C. There was no way she was going to admit that she was accepting the invitation, and so soon, because she wanted to see Nate again.

It was the real reason, though.

Having had quite an interesting talk with Ava after Casey squealed on Nate about the Triple C's infiltration of The North Pole Outlet, Roxy knew she needn't call ahead to see if Nate was in his office. Although the warehouse and shipping sections took weekends off, the 800-number operators and Nate would be in on Saturday.

According to Ava, the man was a workaholic. Roxy understood that. She was one herself. Nate spent more time in his office, in the warehouse, taking calls himself on the 24-hour line and dealing with his own suppliers than he did at home. Roxy would have done the same except for the fact that her home office was larger and less cluttered than the one in the shop. She might be at home, but if she wasn't sleeping, she was working.

Nate's habits made calling for an appointment a detail she could thankfully avoid. She did call the Outlet to let Bridget know where she would be if needed, then headed for the Triple C.

The evening before had been nasty, Old Man Winter throwing a temper tantrum of the worst kind. It was still cold, but briskly so. The wind was less violent, nearly tamed, and the ground was hard beneath a covering of new-fallen snow. On the car radio, Michael Bolton crooned a sexy "White Christmas" and Roxy sang along softly so as not to drown out the poignant notes Michael hit. Usually she tried to outsing the radio, but her pensiveness over the coming interview with Nate acted like a volume control. Would he be angry with her for slipping away rather than confront him under the mistletoe again?

She hoped there wasn't any of the stuff hanging up in his office.

Wondered just how many cases of it were stored within a few feet of his office.

Roxy saw the sign a block away—a tasteful, very noticeable white one with green letters shadowed in red. "Carrington," she noted with approval, was a third the size of "Christmas Catalog." She saw it as an indication that Nate's ego was healthy but not inflated. She'd always liked the sleigh runnerlike swoop of the *C* in Christmas, feeling that the graphic let the most important word hold center stage.

Christmas had always been important to her. Always would be.

And the feeling had absolutely nothing to do with her business. It was simply a magical time of year. A wonderful season in which to fall in love.

Which she was *not* doing, even if she couldn't shake Nate free from her mind.

Roxy parked her car, gathered her courage and walked inside the wide, welcoming doors of the Triple C.

Friday had dawned so full of hope, Nate thought as he leaned back in his chair, his feet on his desk, and helped himself to a fresh, therapeutic Toll House cookie. In fact, the day had built up nicely to the mistletoe episode, where it had hit an incredible high. He'd actually left the Outlet whistling "Deck the Halls" while writing mental memos ordering mistletoe fixed in every doorway at Carrington's Christmas Catalog—although he couldn't think of a one of his own employees that he would like to kiss beneath the snippet of greenery.

But Roxy—now there was a woman he definitely wanted another shot at. After giving the order to have six cartons of the constellation ornaments loaded into one of the smaller delivery vans, Nate had moved on, confident that he would be spending a lot more time in Roxy's company.

That was when things had begun going wrong. Ava called the office to tell him she wouldn't be back at her desk even part-time until after the holidays—they'd asked her if she could work full-time at the Outlet and she'd said yes. She even sounded pleased with the idea, which was very un-Ava-like. Then the temperature had dropped drastically, nosediving in an hour's time into the teens in the wake of an Arctic wind, and he discovered what the usual driver had known for a week already—that the heater didn't work in this particular van. Roxy had left by the time he returned to the Outlet, and didn't answer when he'd tried to call her at home. Dejected, he'd gone home himself only to hear on the evening news that all scheduled high-school sporting events had been canceled for the evening, many simply dropping back a day, contingent on a change in the weather.

Having his day slip right into the gutter had left him in what Ava would call a ''snit''—if Ava were around to say it. Nate began to feel put-upon, taken for granted. Ignored. Football deprivation had been inevitable in the end.

Saturday hadn't dawned nearly as bright, despite the fact that his sister had delivered the batch of foil-wrapped cookies he was now eating. When he'd unwrapped the treats, half of them had been broken. What else could go wrong?

Lots, he decided, upon seeing Wally's face beaming at him from the newspaper again. The giant jolly old fellow was up to something, no doubt about it. But what? There was no call for Santa figures at the hospital outside of the holidays. Clowns visited the rest of the year. Or very large bunnies. He couldn't quite see Wally in a bunny suit, so it was doubtful the man had taken a job elsewhere yet.

Which left Pruitt in contention between Roxy and himself, Nate decided, and he'd lost interest in hiring a man in a red suit. Oh, the idea had let a burst of longed-for adrenaline surge through him once, but since pursuing Roxy gave him a bigger one, Wally could board the next sleigh to the frozen North with his blessing. But not until Roxy was his.

Nate took another cookie and absentmindedly munched on it. Perhaps he should go visit Pruitt one more time to tell him exactly what he wanted under his Christmas tree this year. Nate supposed a lot of guys had asked for the same present, though perhaps not in the same petite, russet-haired package.

Barring that, he could wish on a star; wish just to see

her again. How did the rhyme go? "Star light, star bright…"

As if conjured by the thought—although few stars showed themselves at ten in the morning—his wish came true.

Roxy walked into his office.

Nate jolted forward in his seat so fast, he nearly spilled the plate of cookies off the corner of his desk.

"Hi," she greeted with a warm smile. "The offer of that tour still open?"

"You bet."

She looked wonderful, but then when didn't he think that? She certainly looked none the worse for their all-too-brief dalliance the day before. Did that mean she hadn't, as he'd hoped, shed a few tears while regretting missing his second visit? Yeah, right. Her eyes were clear and glowing rather than puffy and sunken. She'd flounced off then, carelessly going her own way while, to ease his smarting ego, he'd spent considerable time concocting plausible—and implausible—reasons why she'd been gone.

He wouldn't ask her why she'd left her shop the day before, Nate promised himself. For all he knew, she'd had a nearly forgotten dental appointment, or been abducted by aliens. It was none of his business, and the truth was probably tame when compared to his imaginings. Pressing her about it would make him sound nosy, possessive, and—

"What happened to you yesterday?" he asked, deaf to his inner counsel.

Roxy shrugged her shoulders, slipping free of her coat, and gave Nate a wry grin as he stood and came around the desk to help her. "Spooked, I guess."

Nate felt some of the stiffness ease out of his shoulders.

"Spooked" he could relate to. "Yeah, that kiss threw me for a loop at first, too."

"Yeah?"

"Yeah," he said and leered theatrically at her as he tossed her coat over the back of a side chair. "Want to try it again?"

Roxy's smile widened, brightened, softened. "Later?" she suggested.

The knot in his stomach dissolved. "Later," Nate agreed. Standing next to her was making him feel almost as awkward as he'd been in the eighth grade when he'd asked homecoming attendant Mary Jo Atherton to the movies. She'd turned him down. He hoped Roxy wouldn't again.

"Thanks for the ornaments," she said.

So it was going to be business, huh? He could play that game. Play it damn well.

"You're welcome," Nate said. "It was my pleasure to foist them on you. Have a seat."

She was so pretty, her bright hair wisping free beneath the tugged-down bulk of a cream-colored knit stocking cap, her cheeks still rosy from the cold air, her eyes glowing warmly as they met his.

Until exactly how much "later" did he have to wait before kissing her again?

"I do have another reason for coming by this soon," Roxy continued, taking the chair he indicated. "I'm thinking of starting a new branch of Outlet services and don't want to take stock off the sales floor at this time of year to do what needs to be done."

Nate leaned back against his desk as she told him what she wanted to accomplish in redoing The Midas Touch's Christmas tree. He saw ample opportunity in her expansive plans to take her to dinner at a posh place every night for the remainder of the holiday season. Perhaps even lunch, too. Since she was offering to get the supplies from the Triple C, he would call all those shared meals "scouting for clients" rather than "courting." Courting it would be, though. Courting both Roxy and her business. Even as down as he'd been the night before, he'd made one major decision—Roxy was going to be a part of his life this coming year, and so was The North Pole Outlet.

When he was around her, the old adrenaline of challenge flowed in his veins again. The suggestions he'd made for her shop had been created on the spur of the moment, but they'd been viable, doable, profit-building. Exciting. He'd liked the challenge, liked that he'd been able to meet it. What was it Roxy's head clerk had said the other day? Something about the Triple C having an outlet of their own for walk-in traffic. He hadn't considered it at the time, but he was doing so now.

He knew mail order; not face-to-face retailing, though. From cruising Roxy's place, he recognized that he didn't have the expertise to run a remainders shop. But Roxy did. He wanted to formulate a more detailed plan or two before consulting her.

One on a remainders store and one on winning her.

His warehouse aside, he wanted Roxy on a personal level. Sure, he'd only known her for a few days. They'd been intense days, though. That had to count for something.

"So for this test run, I want to keep with the legend of Midas' touch and maximize the opulence by having different shapes, different textures, different materials, yet keep everything gilded," Roxy finished, outlining her tree-trimming strategy.

"A variety of golden ornaments, hmm?" Nate mused,

mentally reviewing his inventory. Especially the remainders stock. "Any special size?"

"All sizes," Roxy said. "If I remember correctly, didn't you have..."

Every word was pure honey to his ears. She knew the stock his firm offered nearly as well as he did. It was a marriage made in heaven.

Marriage?

Slow down there, Carrington. Let's not get carried away.

"It's a big tree, Nate," Roxy said. "Even at wholesale prices, I'm figuring I'll need close to three hundred dollars' worth of decorations. More if I can convince the café to expand the theme into the rest of the restaurant. We could be looking at a thousand."

Which she would probably triple when she billed the restaurant using the principle of cost-plus-time-plus-profit. Nate studied Roxy closely as she went into further detail. Yes, there were definitely dollar signs dancing in her lovely legal-tender-green eyes. He recognized them well, having seen them ring up in other women's eyes. But these dollar signs hadn't been put there by thoughts of *his* income. Roxy was talking personally accrued profit.

Talk about sexy!

Nate pushed to his feet. "We won't have a bit of trouble filling the order immediately, even delivering it to you at the restaurant," he promised. "When do you need it all?"

For the first time since she'd walked in his door, Roxy looked sheepish. "Sunday night?" she suggested. "I know your delivery staff is off, but once the restaurant closes, Bridget and I need to set up our ladders and get to work. Fortunately our new hire agreed to fill extra hours at the Outlet to free us both up. Ava's a marvel of efficiency.''

Nate caught himself before agreeing. So that was why his executive assistant was staying put. Or at least, the reason she would give him. He had a sneaking suspicion that Ava was enjoying herself.

Obviously he didn't know her as well as he'd once thought.

But it also meant that Ava had just moved herself out of a job as his right hand. When she came back to the Triple C after the holidays, he was booting her out—right into the thick of planning and ultimately running Carrington's Christmas-clearance shop. He'd been calling himself the company president for a long time now. It was time to have a vice president, and in Ava he couldn't have found a better one.

Nate grabbed an order book and, taking Roxy's hand, pulled her to her feet. "Come on," he said. "Let's go shopping.''

"You know," Roxy said, letting her hand rest in his as they headed for the warehouse proper, "I've been wondering. If you didn't advertise the constellation ornaments in your clearance flyer because of insufficient stock, just what do you do with such merchandise? Isn't it prohibitive to keep it in stock?''

"Very," Nate answered. "Which is why we destroy most of it rather than store it.''

Roxy winced at the idea. "Destroy it? But holiday decorations are all so beautiful. Magically beautiful," she added.

He knew exactly what she meant. Which was why, although inventory control demanded it, he hadn't been able to crush the constellation ornaments. They'd been too exquisite, too lovely.

"Not all of it is hot," Nate said and stopped to indicate a stack of cartons marked with large *X*'s. He opened one and reached inside. "Some are bad judgment calls. This, for instance."

The ornament Nate held in his hand was a three-dimensional star painted the most atrocious glow-in-the-dark pink he'd ever seen. The supplier had promised soft cotton-candy pink, then had abruptly gone out of business after delivering punk pink in its place. Even offering the stars at two for a dollar in the flyer hadn't drawn in more than a handful of takers. "This," he said, "is an ornament that deserves death."

Roxy took it from him, holding it lightly in her hand. Nate found he adored the look of concentration on her face. "It's nicely made," she determined. "Very nicely made. And different. I like that about it."

He was sure he'd heard her wrong. "You like it?"

"I could like it," she said and chewed her bottom lip in thought. "I could like it a lot. How many do you think you have?"

Far too many. "Why?" Nate asked, looking at the ornament closely. What possibilities did Roxy see in it that he hadn't?

She grinned up at him. "Because," she said as she tossed the horrible pink star in the air, then caught it one-handed, "if you've got three gross of them—"

He had a lot more than that.

"And you spray paint half of them glorious gold and the other half snowy white and then dust them all with fine-grain, pearlized glitter, I'll take them." Roxy's smile widened impishly. "For fifty cents per piece."

"Seventy-five apiece," Nate countered. "I've got to add the cost of paint, glitter and labor but I'll throw in shipping for free."

"Done," Roxy said. Mischievous delight danced with the dollar signs in her eyes.

She was the most desirable woman he'd ever known in his entire life. She took his breath away.

She offered him her hand, ready to seal their agreement.

He had a much better idea. Snaking his arm around Roxy's waist, he bundled her close and kissed her. Kissed her quite decently.

As a kiss, it deserved a place of honor in the Lovers' Hall of Fame. Cleopatra and Mark Antony hadn't shared a kiss like this. Romeo and Juliet? Not a chance. Lancelot and Guinevere? No way.

Roxy marveled that she was the lucky woman to experience it, to share in it, to return it. Considering Nate had the ability to make her knees go weak, her toes curl, and her mind dissolve, she wondered how he had eluded capture by a marriage-minded huntress. Even a nonmarriage-minded huntress. He looked great, especially in his midnight-blue company sweatshirt and faded jeans, his sandy hair falling in his eyes. He smelled wonderful—like scented candles, pine air spray, plastic bubble wrap and chocolate-chip cookies. He tasted like the cookies—a quite erotic taste it was, too. She could easily go on kissing him forever.

His arm drew her tighter against him, flattening her breasts against his chest. Or had that been her pressing nearer him? It was difficult to tell with her arms around him, with his arms around her. His mouth was hot and greedy—or was that hers? Roxy tilted her head back against his forearm and Nate responded, melding them even closer together. She hadn't removed her stocking cap before, but he tugged it free, dropping it to the warehouse floor, letting her hair spill over her shoulders, down her back. When he buried his hands in it, Roxy sighed with ecstasy.

Nate chuckled, the sound deep, sensuous and eloquently wicked, Roxy thought.

"I never thought of business as an aphrodisiac before," he said, each softly murmured word acting as a further caress against her sensitized lips.

Replete with the unexpected rush of pleasure, Roxy felt incapable of words. He was right. Both times they'd kissed, they'd been talking shop beforehand, making suggestions on how to improve each other's business. It had been seductive, erotic.

It had been foreplay.

At the thought, Roxy eased away from Nate. If she continued in this vein, she knew exactly where she would end the weekend—and it wasn't on a ladder at The Midas Touch Café.

It was too soon to take the next step in this rather strange relationship. They were rivals, both determined to hire Walter Pruitt. They were competitors since both vied for customers' holiday business—Carrington's sold retail to the public as well as wholesale to Christmas shops. But, at the rate they were going, there was no doubt about it. She and Nate would end up lovers.

At the realization, a chill of anticipation ran up Roxy's spine. They had only kissed and yet the earth had done some determined shimmying beneath her feet. If—when—they made love, it would get down and rock and roll.

"Ornaments, remember?" she said and ticked off the required items on her fingers. "Gilded apples, gilded pears, gilded stars. At least five dozen each. Wired ribbon, probably ten yards or more."

"God, I love the scale in which you think," Nate said

with feeling as he scribbled quickly on the order form. "Tell you what. I'll give you a five-percent discount if you pay within ten days."

Roxy nearly melted on the spot. Oh, talk about foreplay! "Done!" she cried.

"Not nearly," Nate declared and tossed aside his order book to seal the deal with another kiss.

Already addicted to this way of doing business with him, Roxy kissed Nate back.

Loath to let Roxy leave, Nate called in a lunch order to a nearby Chinese restaurant that delivered, then filled the time until the chow mein arrived with an expanded tour of the Triple C facility. He'd given other women large-scale look-sees at his place, but not a one had asked detailed questions about how the operation ran. Roxy not only did so, but she suggested he look into the creation of a Carrington credit card to augment the major credit-card companies the shopping public could now use. "After all," she'd reasoned, "you make extra by charging interest on business accounts that are ninety-days overdue—" He had a lot of those. "Why not be able to make some interest on smaller charge orders, too?"

Nate could barely wait until Monday when he could set Casey to tracking down the most accommodating bank handling private-issue cards.

The sun had bullied its way past the clouds by midafternoon although the temperature had not improved. Which was fine with Nate. If it warmed up too much, it would make the football field one gigantic mud slide and he wanted Adams High to win the rescheduled game that night through skill, not mud-slicked luck. He had bet Casey twenty bucks that Wayne Huffman would quarterback the team to a five-point-or-more win over their rivals. Casey had bet that the win would be by less. Neither of them ever bet against their alma mater, but Nate's own experience on the field had led him to make a comfortable bit of change over his ex-basketball-playing friend.

Ever since they'd gotten out of college and returned to their hometown, the two of them had been loyal Adams High boosters, attending all the home games and some of those away, as well. And, although the games were nearly always played on a Friday, not a single one of the women either had ever dated had managed to split the two apart on game night.

Until now.

Fortunately Roxy would never know she'd accomplished such a feat. She would never hear it from him, Nate knew, and Casey valued the seat that the coach saved for Cannon-Arm Carrington and his buddy on the fifty-yard line too much to ever blab. Nate doubted Roxy would appreciate the sacrifice Casey was about to make in giving up his ticket to the game that night, but since the high-school football stadium was a very nonbusiness place to take her, Nate was appropriating his friend's season ticket.

Football. It was not only the most perfect sport ever invented, it had nothing in common with the holiday season but the time of year. In going to the game with him, Roxy would realize that it was *her* he was interested in, not Wally Pruitt. There would be no one to even faintly remind her of their elusive Mr. Kringle. Although a couple of the players were big guys, not one approached the height and breadth of Wally, and the school band's lone tuba player went against type in being Ichabod Crane-thin.

Football. It was a brilliant move on his part to take her to the game. This was not only a great first date, this was wholesome, this was American.

This was the act of a desperate man. He sure hoped she would agree to go.

"I've got tickets to the Adams High game tonight," Nate said as he paid the delivery guy for the Chinese takeout. "How about going with me?"

"Sorry, dude," the delivery kid said, "but I went to Southside and Adams was like our hated rival."

"Not you," Nate corrected and jerked his head in Roxy's direction. "Her."

"Whoa, I'm like relieved, man. Thought you were asking me to the game instead of givin' me a tip," the kid said and beat a hasty retreat, as if he expected Nate to reclaim the tip Nate had passed him.

"Me?" Roxy asked, her eyes wide and startled at the invitation. She took the carton of fluffy white rice Nate handed her and studied him for a moment. "You're serious."

"Yep," Nate agreed, fishing around in the delivery bag for the accompanying plastic flatware. "It should be a good game. The quarterback's got a great arm and—"

"Nate," Roxy said. "It's December. It's cold outside—*really* cold outside. There's a chance of snow again and the temperatures are due to stay way below freezing."

It sounded like primo football weather to him. "Yeah," Nate agreed, waiting for her to get to the downside of his suggestion. He hadn't thought there was one.

"And you want me to go out in these rather nasty elements with you, sit on hard, unsheltered stadium seats and watch teenage boys try to trample each other into the turf?" Roxy asked.

He began to think going to the game might not have been one of his more brilliant plays. "Yeah?" he answered, hopeful yet beginning to rethink his position just in case. There were still those upscale restaurants to check out, but he hated to miss the game.

Roxy helped herself to the chow mein, spooning it over the rice in her carton before dazzling him with a particularly warm smile. "I'd love to go," she said.

If he hadn't been in love with her before, Nate figured he was now. Dead and gone in love. It didn't feel as uncomfortable as he'd feared, either. In fact, it felt great. Really great!

7

It was early afternoon when Roxy pulled out of the Triple C's parking lot. It was being surrounded by literally tons of holiday decorations that had held her in thrall—not that she'd found it difficult to leave Nate—that had kept her dawdling. Even as she worded it in her mind, Roxy didn't believe the excuse. Not that she needed one. Her staff probably hadn't missed her at all back at the shop. With the season in full swing, the Outlet ran itself. And when things slackened off, Bridget handled things.

Perhaps that was why she'd felt dissatisfied lately, Roxy mused. She wasn't as needed as she had once been. She'd delegated the responsibilities that used to keep her so connected to her business. She still chose and ordered the stock, but the matching she did of invoices to packing slips was done out of a curiosity to know what had come in. Casey and his bookkeepers rechecked details, issued payments, followed through on returns and handled all payroll transactions. Bridget supervised the Outlet employees, hired and fired them when necessary, scheduled hours and dealt with time sheets. The only thing Roxy hadn't assigned elsewhere yet was advertising, and even that was in the process of being handed over to an agency. In a way, she'd nearly delegated herself out of a job.

And yet there wasn't a single responsibility she wanted

to take back. They hadn't been the fun things; those she had kept for herself—the ordering and the sales-floor layout planning. She worked long hours at both, but only because she drew out the time, savoring it.

Filling the empty hours of her life.

That was all about to end. She was really enthusiastic about the new decorating service. Forming it had crystallized her thoughts on expansion—she was definitely buying out the travel agency's lease and increasing the Outlet's square footage. She would be able to implement Nate's suggestion about layaway on higher-priced items and create a separate storage lockup for the new purchasing plan. Then there was the Ornament-a-Month Club to begin. With a little luck, the expanded space and promotions would generate an increase in business to fund a second store in eighteen to twenty-four months.

Roxy walked into the Outlet barely conscious of the buzz of activity around her. Her mind flitted from Nate to forming new business plans and back to Nate again. To separate him from thoughts of her business was now difficult. He not only functioned as a supplier, he had become an idea man.

A delightful idea man. Oh, sure, she'd once been suspicious of him—and with good reason. He had, after all, sent Ava in to spy on her. But Nate's brand of industrial espionage hadn't been to steal business from the Outlet, just to make off with Wally Pruitt. And Wally wasn't, as yet, one of her employees, so Roxy was willing to forgive Nate. Particularly since she'd gained a hard worker in Ava.

Roxy was still determined to best Nate in pursuit of Wally. Since neither of them had made headway, they really should push the pink-slipped Santa to make up his mind. The season was passing quickly. Soon it wouldn't matter if Kriss Kringle sat enthroned on the small dais in the back of her shop.

When the Outlet's former Santa had taken off to warmer climes, his usual throne had been converted into a display area. As she'd been expecting to acquire a new Santa, moving the heavy chair from its dais had seemed unnecessary to Roxy. Instead she'd filled the chair with a basket of elegantly frosted pinecones and had layered red, green, white and gold linens along the chair back.

Roxy glanced around, wondering where she was most needed, and found Ava bearing down on her determinedly.

Ava's appearance had changed drastically since her first days at the Outlet. After learning from Casey that Ava was in Nate's employ, Roxy had confronted the woman. Rather than ask her to leave, Roxy had requested that Ava stay on through the season. Although she'd been planted at the Outlet as a spy, Ava was willing to do whatever was needed and was a marvel of efficiency. She was just what was needed during the rushed final days of the holiday season, especially with the new decorating service to be launched.

Ava had agreed to stay the remaining weeks. Had even agreed not to tell Nate that Roxy knew of his attempt at espionage. However, the next time Ava had come in, Roxy had barely recognized her. Gone was the gray-haired mouse Bridget had hired. In her place was a stunning, mature blonde in a tailored business suit. Ava looked exactly what she was, the executive assistant of a successful man. She even carried a leather-bound note-book with her, jotting down notes in it as she dealt with customers. Although she was a relative newcomer to the Outlet, her work performance had continued to be beyond belief. The only thing that irked the rest of the staff was that Ava managed to find reasons to shed her official Outlet apron at every opportunity. The apron was missing now, but her name tag was in place on the breast pocket of her suit jacket. While the other staff members had temporarily adopted the names of Santa's reindeer, Ava's name tag read Ms. Ava.

"What did you think of the Triple C?" Ava asked, pride in Nate's company ringing in her voice.

Roxy grinned, thinking more of the company's founder than of the warehouse-cum-office. "Awesome," she said. "I wanted to dig in all those packing cases like they were holiday presents."

"We have a quantity of lovely items there," Ava agreed. "But you do here, too."

Roxy nearly giggled at the politely condescending words. "Well, I think we do," she said, "but—"

"Excuse me," a customer interrupted. The woman gestured to the dais at the back of the shop. "Can you tell me why there is no Santa here this year?"

Roxy kept a pleasant smile on her face with difficulty. She remembered this woman well. An Amazon in build and bluster, she was a regular holiday-season visitor to the Outlet. One whose children monopolized Santa for half an hour before she dragged them off, never bothering to buy even a token piece of merchandise.

"I count on this store," the woman continued, the chip on her shoulder nearly visible. "There is always a shorter line to see Santa, and I'm not forced to purchase one of those hideous pictures of my kids seated on his lap."

Hard-pressed to retain her smile, Roxy looked at the children standing on either side of the obnoxious Amazon and made an effort to sound cheerful for their sakes. "I'm sorry, but Santa couldn't make it this year," she told the youngsters.

"Mr. Claus has a very full schedule," Ava added officiously. "Corporate matters, you see. If you'd like, I would be glad to pass on any word the children cared to leave."

Surprised at the glibness of Ava's reply, Roxy waited for the Amazon to turn away in a huff, dragging her hapless children with her.

Instead, the boy lifted his chin in a challenge and addressed Ava. "Who are you?" he demanded, his expression and tone of voice mulish.

A definite chip off the mother block, Roxy thought. At school he was probably the bully who demanded other kids' lunch money as tribute.

Ava sized the boy up and down coolly. "I'm Mr. Claus's executive assistant," she announced, all adult and all business. There would be no bending of Ava's stiffened backbone, Roxy knew. There wasn't a bit of willow in the able woman's makeup; she was oak through and through. Roxy actually found the real Ava—as opposed to the gray-haired infiltrator—rather intimidating.

"I am making five-minute appointments to listen to toy requests *good* children wish relayed to Mr. Claus," Ava said and lifted her ever-present notebook and pen. "I have an opening at two-twenty if you are interested."

The time scheduled was nearly thirty minutes away. It was also the time of Ava's scheduled break. As far as Roxy was concerned, the Amazon's kid deserved nothing but a lump of coal for Christmas, yet here was Ava volunteering to give up her break time to listen to his toy demands. They would definitely be demands from a kid like him.

"Perhaps in the interim your mother will buy a new tree ornament for each of you," Ava suggested, her eagle eye now trained on the disagreeable woman. "You can show them to me when we have our meeting and I can describe each to Mr. Claus when I meet with him later today.''

Her admiration for Nate's assistant growing by reindeerlike leaps, Roxy made a snap decision. Within the hour, Ava was settled on the dais, perched on the red velvet cushioned throne, her ever-ready notebook resting on an ornately carved cherry writing desk Roxy had appropriated from the nearby Victorian display area. Wide-eyed children sat in a half circle before her, each taking a turn—or rather their prescheduled appointment time—to describe their behavior over the past year and request a single toy. Ava wouldn't allow for more—Mr. Claus did like to leave some surprises, she insisted.

"This is so clever," a mother declared, sidling up to Roxy as she watched "Ms. Ava" in action. "Other places have had mechanical reindeer, teenagers dressed as elves, even Santa's extremely plump wife. None of them very nineties, if you know what I mean. But this—this is very updated." She grinned and lowered her voice. "It's also giving me time to shop without worrying about what my kids might be touching! Thank whoever's idea this was."

Should she thank Ava for stepping in? Roxy wondered. Or Nate for placing Ava undercover at the Outlet?

Up on Santa's dais, a six-year-old girl faced the attentive-but-nonsmiling Ava without a qualm. "And, Ms. Ava, I've *even* been nice to the baby brother Mr. Claus brought me last year even though I *didn't* ask for him."

Roxy didn't wait to hear Ava's answer to that one. She'd just realized something was missing—treats. Over a month before, she'd bought sugar-free candy canes for Santa to distribute to the children. Dashing back to the break room, she grabbed up several bags of them. Yet halfway back to the dais, she realized it was entirely out of character for an executive assistant to hand out candy and hastily grabbed one of the younger staff members and told her to get rid of her apron. The girl's mouth almost dropped open in shock at such a request. But to fill the position of elfin office clerk and assist Mr. Claus's trusted associate, Ms. Ava, the scarlet apron had to go.

"Ah, Ms. Cupid," Ava murmured, addressing the girl by the name on her identification badge as Roxy brought her to the dais. "Would you be so good as to make all further appointments for the young ladies and gentlemen? Mr. Claus so hates to hear of pushing and shoving in line."

The children who had been fidgeting, anxiously waiting their turn to join the charmed circle at Ava's feet, stilled at the mention of the august Mr. Claus's name. Roxy ran off to get a blank "appointment" book and pen. It looked as if she no longer had a need for Wally Pruitt at the Outlet.

Of course, she thought, smiling to herself, there was no reason Nate needed to know that. No reason at all.

The snow started an hour after Roxy had left the Triple C. By the time Nate turned into the Outlet's lot, the white stuff blanketed houses, streets and cars parked at the shopping centers. He passed two kids already trying to make a snowman out of the inch of new accumulation. They would be lucky to build Frosty a foot tall before they turned into Popsicles themselves, he thought. It was damn cold.

The heater in his Corvette was going full blast. In the back, he'd shoved heavy stadium blankets, stadium cushions and a tall thermos of coffee. Roxy would not, he vowed, regret going to the game with him. She would be as toasty as it was possible to be.

He'd even thought to bring a flask of brandy, should stronger antifreeze be needed, although cuddling her in his arms had an appeal that the spirits couldn't match.

He was ready to kill time waiting for her at the shop, even willing to miss the kickoff, but the pace of the place had slowed to a near crawl now that it was dinnertime. The store's location at the corner of the strip mall allowed it to look a bit like a gingerbread house from the outside—and a warmly glowing one, at that. There were far fewer cars drawn into the lot by the ambience than had been there earlier. Ava's car, he noted, was absent. He was relieved that she'd left for the day already. She'd given him one hell of a suspicious look the last time he'd been there. He'd half expected her to call and demand to know what new plan he was implementing. Just in case, he'd been leery of checking his voice mail at the office and had monitored the calls he got at home through the answering machine. Ava hadn't tried to get hold of him.

Which didn't bode well, now that he thought about it.

Nate didn't have to consider his executive assistant's reaction for long. As if she'd been on the watch for him, Roxy slipped out of the store and headed for his car. Unable to react quickly enough, Nate was forced to lean across and open the passenger's door from the inside rather than play the perfect gentleman and open it for her from the outside.

She looked delightful, bundled up in her long camel-colored coat. Her russet curls spilled around her shoulders from beneath the same creamy stocking cap she'd worn earlier. A matching scarf was wrapped around her neck and mittens covered her long, gracefully narrow hands.

"Hi!" Roxy greeted, smiling as she slipped inside the Corvette quickly and shut the door behind her.

The moment the car's inner light went out, Nate gave

in to temptation. He leaned over and kissed her lightly. It was probably only in his imagination that Roxy's lips clung to his a moment longer than the brief, friendly, non-threatening nature of the caress demanded. His voice dropping unconsciously to a deeper, fuller, intimate tone, Nate said, ''Hi.''

Roxy felt warmed all over, and not because she'd added extra layers of clothing. Nate had an incredibly sexy voice. It wrapped around her like a soft, comforting co-coon, making her feel special. She liked the feeling.

She'd liked that brief, tantalizing kiss, too. Looked forward to the longer, hotter kiss that would no doubt con-clude the evening.

Roxy settled herself in the bucket seat, locking the seat belt in place. ''I haven't been to a football game in a long time,'' she said. ''How did you know I love them?''

In the process of putting the car in motion, Nate nearly stripped the gears, caught off guard by the blatant lie.

One he fell for as she'd hoped. ''This is high-school football, not the pros,'' he reminded.

''It's more than that. It's your old school,'' Roxy said.

Nate glanced over at her, further astonishment over her statement sending his eyebrows soaring up and out of sight beneath his tumbling hair. No doubt about it. Before the night was over, she would be burying her fingers in that angel-hair-fine mass.

''How'd you know that?'' he asked, clearly stunned.

Roxy gave him a smug grin. ''I checked you out. Called Casey. He was most informative.'' He didn't have to know that today hadn't been the day she'd twisted the accountant's arm.

Nate concentrated on his driving, turning off the major roadway into an older residential area, weaving his way toward the school grounds. "I suppose you know my shoe size by now, then," he said ruefully.

"Almost," Roxy agreed, giving him a mischievous grin. "I've known for some time that you are so unsure over which of us Wally Pruitt will choose that you resorted to industrial espionage."

"Oh."

He was being careful, not giving anything away. Wondering, no doubt, just how much information Casey had willingly sacrificed to keep her business.

Delighted with the way things were going, Roxy relaxed and enjoyed the glitter of the yard decorations along their route. "Ava is a miracle. I'm surprised you can do without her for even a couple of weeks."

He didn't pretend ignorance over her statement, which pleased Roxy. She liked that he didn't apologize for being belatedly honest. "A couple of weeks? It's only been three days since she signed on with you," Nate said.

"Four, counting today," Roxy corrected. "She's a hard worker. Efficient. Always on time."

"A saint," he agreed and slanted a look at her. "Without Ava, the Triple C would still be a chump-change business, regional rather than national. She knows it and still lets me take all the glory for our success."

Roxy doubted that Ava would agree with him, but she thought better of Nate for crediting his assistant and being sincere as he did so. She wondered if he really knew Ava as well as he thought. No one meeting the woman would ever have guessed she was a great actress. Since sinking her teeth into the part of Mr. Claus's executive assistant and spending the afternoon talking to children, Ava had shown a completely different side of her personality.

"Planting her in my shop hasn't helped you get a jump on luring Wally away from me, has it," Roxy said.

Although he was looking straight ahead, keeping his eyes on the slush-slicked road, Roxy could see that Nate's smile widened. "You really have a one-track mind, don't you? Business isn't everything, Rox. But football—do you really like the game?"

What she really liked was being with him, but she had no intention of telling him so. The sensation was too new to admit aloud. It needed evaluation, so as she'd assisted shoppers, she'd thought about how alive she felt around him and had arrived at no logical answer. It needed research so she'd agreed to go to the football game with him, lying only a little about her appreciation of the game—okay, a lot—just to be in his company and collect data she could mull over later at her leisure.

Perhaps she was just coming down with a rare virus and the rush of blood in her ears when she was around him was merely a symptom, a foreshadowing of time to be spent in bed.

Although she'd thought him an attractive fellow at first sight, she'd only noticed her heightened awareness of him at The Midas Touch Café. Oh, sure, he'd helped her a little in getting a better table, but was that reason enough to keep thinking about him? No, it wasn't.

But it was. Numerous times in the past week she'd mentally relived the minutes she'd spent in his company, heard again the amusement and the authority in his voice, seen again the steel in his eyes when they'd leveled on the maître d'. Reveled again at the warmth in those same eyes when they rested on her. The mistletoe, the business ideas she planned to implement...

Roxy stole a look at Nate's profile as he told her in unnecessary detail about Adams High's season record thus far. There was something musical about his voice—perhaps it was just the enthusiasm that rang in the deep tones, the pleasure he was obviously taking from regaling her with sports statistics that was endearing. Her eyes lingered on the finely sculpted lines of his jaw and his lips, and she remembered that surprising, all-too-brief kiss he'd given her in greeting.

Perhaps that foreshadowed time in bed had nothing to do with the flu.

The evening was turning out better than he'd ever anticipated, Nate thought as he watched Roxy jump to her feet with excitement as the Adams team brought down the enemy ball-carrying hulk. He hadn't totally believed her when she'd told him she loved football. It was sweet of her to tell him so, but he'd noticed a certain telltale glazing of her eyes when he'd given her the brief rundown on the season on their way to the game. Whether she had fibbed or not, Roxy was obviously enjoying herself now. And so was he. More than he could have believed possible.

On their trek from the parking lot, Roxy had insisted upon carrying the stadium cushions, hugging them tightly to her chest, while he tossed the blankets over his shoulder and gathered up the thermos of coffee. When she'd slipped on an icy spot, he'd put his arm around her shoulders to steady her step and she'd slipped her free arm companionably around his waist. Perhaps because it was so cold, she sat close to him on the seat in the stands, the two of them sharing warmth. There was a lot more than just warmth he wanted to share but he wasn't going to rush things. At least not by much. She was a gorgeous woman and, not being a fool—most of the time—he wanted her. Wanted to make love to her, with her. Cozy up to her on as many cold, wintry nights as he possibly could.

But desire wasn't all he was feeling. In fact, love wasn't all he was feeling, either. He liked her. Honestly *liked* her, which was something new for him where attractive women were concerned. So he hoped the happy glow in Roxy's eyes wasn't due entirely to her enthusiasm for the game. He wanted her to both love and like him, too. Truth was, he was enjoying her company more than the game. Which was another admission that even under torture he would never let slip to Casey or any of the other guys he met regularly at the sports bar at playoff time.

Although the game was nearly over, Nate caught Roxy watching him again, looking for clues on how to respond to plays out on the field. She hadn't the foggiest idea of what was going on, yet she'd agreed to come to the game with him. Had wheedled information out of Casey about him.

Nate didn't think Roxy's doing so had anything to do with business, even if she made it sound like it had. The thought gave him an odd sensation in his chest—a little like indigestion, but a nice kind of indigestion.

"Is there any coffee left?" she asked, shivering as she snuggled closer to him.

The pseudo-indigestion increased, and unexpected warmth spread through his system.

Roxy's eyes were luminous beneath the stadium lights. Was it because he'd added the brandy to the remaining coffee at halftime?

"Still cold?" he asked.

She laughed at him, swept him away with the throaty richness of her voice. "That's a silly question, Nate," she said and drew on an invisible cigarette before breathing a cloud of vapor at him.

If she wasn't careful, he was going to kiss her right

there in the stadium. And not kiss her lightly, but deeply, passionately. A knock-her-socks-off kind of kiss.

"Do you want to leave?" he offered.

Her eyes widened slightly. Gazing into them made him nearly lose track of the game. There were three minutes left to play. Adams had the ball on the ten-yard line, and he was thinking how much better it would be if they were alone in his car. Was regretting the fact that he'd bought a vehicle without a back seat in it.

He had it bad.

Roxy slipped her mittened hand in his. The rival team could have trampled Wayne Huffman and his teammates in the mud and taken the football to the opposite end of the field and Nate wouldn't have noticed. His leather-gloved fingers closed firmly around hers.

"Thank you for coming to the game with me, Rox," Nate murmured.

She glowed. "Thank you for inviting me. It's been fun. I didn't realize you were a legend at Adams until the coach called you 'Cannon-Arm.'"

Some things a fella never lived down. His Uncle Will had been an Adams football man before him and whenever he ran into his former coach, the man invariably greeted him as 'Pony,' the nickname Will had inadvertently earned by running with his head up, like a pony, rather than down when carrying the ball.

On the field the players lined up against each other again. The coaches were letting the clock run out rather than call a time-out. On Adams's side, because they were so far ahead and it was damn cold. On the rivals' side, because they were so far behind and it was damn cold. It was time to move on to phase two in his plan.

"What do you say to sharing a pizza after the game?" Nate suggested.

The hoped-for eager agreement didn't tumble from Roxy's lips. Instead she centered her gaze on the muddy back of young Wayne Huffman as he shouted unintelligible calls to his teammates. "I don't think so," Roxy said, efficiently blasting his plans for the evening all to hell.

Rejection was a fairly instant cure when it came to indigestion of the heart. And the hell of it all was, his male pride demanded he not let her know he'd felt a thing.

The ever-warming look in Nate's eyes was nearly Roxy's undoing. It would be so easy to give in to her attraction to him. Far too easy. She'd spent most of the game being overly aware of Nate's broad, masculine form so close to her on the bench. As subtle as it was, the scent of his aftershave beat out the aromas of coffee, hot dogs and mustard around them. Because it was freezing, she'd stayed close to him to share body warmth—or so she tried to convince herself. When her mind began to fantasize about being even closer to him, being alone with him in front of her living-room fireplace enjoying the flames that licked through her body rather than those burning in the hearth, Roxy knew she had to relinquish such dreams and put distance between them.

It was bad timing that her decision coincided with his offer of pizza after the game. Worse that she hadn't the courage to be honest with him over why she turned him down.

"Hey," she said, giving him a weak—she admitted it— smile and an uneasy glance before gazing back at the kids on the field. "Tomorrow's still a workday for me. With Christmas almost upon us, 'tis not the season for me to be away from the store much." She hoped he didn't remember that she'd spent the majority of the day in his company already and hadn't worried about her shop during one of those minutes. "In fact," Roxy said, "I've got sales receipts to tally yet tonight." When Nate didn't even grunt in understanding, she gave up the pretense of watching the game and turned to him, adding, "I'm sorry."

He wasn't even looking at her. His eyes were trained on the young titans knocking into each other at the end of the field. Men!

"Oof! Did you see that?" Nate demanded. "I'm surprised the ref didn't throw a flag on that play."

She should have known better than to think he'd meant anything by the offer other than that he was hungry, Roxy thought, fuming silently. Here she was going all soft and mushy around him and he was more interested in some blockheaded game where males mangled each other. Sport was just another name for battle—a pastime only a man could possibly find enjoyable.

Roxy shoved her hands deep in the pockets of her coat and tucked her chin into the enveloping comfort of her scarf. The pleasure she'd derived from the evening was lying between them, dead as the squabbled-over pigskin on the field. All she wanted was to be taken back to the Outlet. She would shove the receipts in her briefcase and lug them home so that she had something to do to keep her from thinking about him, because if she lit that dreamed-of fire in the fireplace, she would be gazing into it alone. As usual.

Well, she had what she wanted most. She had The North Pole Outlet. Center on that, she told herself.

Unaware that any overture on his part had become unwelcome, Nate put his arm around her shoulders and hugged her close. "What a game!" he said, a heartless grin stretching the corners of his mouth attractively. "Did you ever see anything like it?"

Apparently the game had ended in a satisfactory malevolent creaming of Adams's opponents.

"Never," Roxy admitted truthfully.

"You sound tired, sweetheart," Nate said.

Oh, endearments now. What next?

"Listen, why don't you let me help you with things at the shop?" he offered. "The pizza could be delivered. I'm not a bad hand with inventory sheets and P&L reports, you know."

His delivery sounded sincere, honest and sensitive. Roxy chose to see Nate's tongue as forked. The snake had been lying through his teeth all night. He hadn't wanted to get to know her, to start over as he'd claimed. He was still bent on that dumb industrial-espionage kick. Wasn't it enough that Ava, his right hand at the Triple C, was firmly ensconced at the Outlet? Now, under the guise of being helpful, Nate wanted to get a look at her books!

Roxy rubbed fretfully at the start of a headache in her temple. Damn it. She'd liked the Nate Carrington he'd been that evening. Liked him even more than the Nate he'd been at The Midas Touch.

It just went to show that a person couldn't be really good at more than one thing. She was good at business—had to be because it looked like she had pretty rotten taste when it came to men.

"It's nice of you to volunteer, but I'll have a better feel for what's selling if I do it myself," Roxy said.

"Another night then," Nate suggested.

"Another night," Roxy echoed, sure that there would never be one. The sooner Wally Pruitt put them out of this endless suspense, the sooner she could get Nate Carrington out of her life.

It would be quite a while before she got him out of her mind.

Out of her heart.

She was an idiot to have let him worm his way into that usually barred organ. At what age did a woman become immune to a roguish grin, to a devil-may-care glint in a man's eyes? Probably only when she was dead and buried.

With her luck, the mating dance would continue in the hereafter. That bright light a woman went toward in her final moments was probably generated by a man with a smile straight off a Bailey and Salazar toothpaste billboard.

Turning down yet another offer—this time a protective "I'll - follow - you - home - to - make - sure - you - get - there - safely" one—Roxy gathered up the stadium cushions while Nate refolded the blankets. The ride back to the Outlet, where she'd left her car, was filled with commentary on the football game. He mentioned specific plays. She made what she felt were appropriate murmurs of agreement in the right places.

Only the security lights in the stores and the parking-lot lights were lit back at the strip mall. As Nate pulled his Corvette into the space next to Roxy's car, she unbuckled her seat belt.

"Thanks for a lovely evening, Nate," she said, the smile pasted on her lips reflecting none of the inner turmoil and hurt she was feeling.

He looked at the mittened hand she offered him, his one eyebrow doing a "You're kidding" rise beneath his tumbling hair. He ignored her hand. "If you don't want me to tail you home," he said, "then humor me by letting me see that you don't get mugged before driving out of the lot."

It was easier to give in than to argue. She couldn't be

angry with him. It wasn't his fault she was attracted to flakes.

And he was the most attractive flake to cross her path in a long, long while. Not just physically, but personality-wise, as well.

Better to be alone than be doomed to a life with such a man, though. That was what her rabidly independent Aunt Charlotte always said. Sometimes it was difficult to agree totally with that declaration, though.

Like now.

Nate didn't wait to see if she was going to humor him, let him play bodyguard for the five minutes or less it would take her to disarm the store security system, grab the paperwork from where her staff had left it on her desk, and reset the alarm. He got out of the car and was around to her side before Roxy managed to find the door latch in the unfamiliar vehicle.

He loomed over her, as darkly threatening as any mugger, but in many ways far more dangerous since he threatened her peace of mind.

Her heart.

8

It hadn't been easy to keep from sounding annoyed as he rambled on about nonexistent plays. Since he'd figured Roxy wouldn't know he was making them up, Nate had talked just to fill the void. Now they were at her shop and she was doing an act on him, pretending that she wasn't giving him the dreaded silent treatment. He didn't know what he'd done to deserve it; he only knew she'd switched the system on. He could practically see the flashing lights that indicated it was armed.

He held the car door for her. She exited as gracefully as the *Nutcracker's* sugarplum fairy. "All right," Roxy said, the lack of enthusiasm in her voice rather chilly to the ear. It made the freezing air temperature seem almost tropical by comparison. "You can wait just inside the shop door while I get my things."

Lackey City, hmm? What exactly had he done? All he could remember was asking her if she wanted pizza. She was the one who'd slammed the invitation back in his face as if she was returning an ill-served handball. Oh, she'd tried to cover, tried to be polite, but he'd heard her withdrawal in the words.

If only he knew what was going on behind those beautiful eyes. They'd turned as unreadable as the first profit-and-loss statement Casey had ever handed him. He'd learned to fathom the P&L. But Roxy wasn't about to let him fathom her. She'd done the equivalent of electrifying the fence and setting the dogs loose to guarantee that he never had a chance.

He hadn't gotten where he was in business without making his own chances, though. He would just have to make one now, Nate decided.

When Roxy opened the main door to her shop, he was right on her heels. She locked it behind them, at least smart enough to know the odds changed on the street after dark.

"I'll be right back," she said and darted off through the shadowed forest of ornament-loaded trees.

Nate counted off five seconds before following her.

"It was only pizza," Nate said, lounging in the doorway of her office.

Roxy wasn't startled by his appearance behind her. He wasn't the kind of man who did what a woman told him to do unless he wanted to. Nate hadn't wanted to wait at the door.

She let the sales receipts lie where they were. Because she didn't trust her hands not to shake and betray her inner turmoil, she pressed them flat against the desktop. "I guess I'm not really hungry for pizza," she said.

"Maybe I'm not, either."

His voice was pitched low so that it fell softly on her ears. Her back still to him, Roxy bit her lip, afraid that some of what she'd been thinking, feeling, would tumble forth rather than remain locked inside.

He crossed the few feet of flooring between them, and let his hands settle on her shoulders. Even through her layers of coat, sweater and silk blouse, she felt the heat of his touch.

"Nate, I—"

His lips brushed the crown of her head. She should have left her stocking cap on rather than automatically toss it aside on a chair. It might have armored her, protected her from such a tender caress.

"Your hair smells of cinnamon and pine," Nate said.

"The shop's aromatic diffuser—"

His hands stayed where they were on her shoulders, but his mouth roamed lower, his breath teasing the nape of her neck. Roxy forgot what she had been about to say. Despite herself, she let her head drop forward, allowing him easier access to the sensitive spot.

"I'm not pushing you, Rox," Nate whispered and kneaded her shoulders slightly.

Wasn't he? She was nearly putty in his hands this very minute.

"There's something between us. Or should be," Nate continued. "You've felt it as much as I have."

She had. Practically from the moment they'd met outside Walter and Marigold Pruitt's front gate.

"This has nothing to do with which of us gets Santa," Nate said.

Roxy twisted, slipping from beneath his touch but not away from the alluring warmth of his body. "Are you so sure, Nate?"

His mouth twisted wryly. "Trust me, Rox. When I'm around you, Wally's the last thing on my mind."

She would berate herself for asking later. She already knew the answer. It thrummed through her with every breath she took. She asked it anyway.

"And what is on your mind, Nate?" she said quietly.

His fingertips brushed along the hollows of her cheeks, slid into her hair, tugging at it slightly so that she tilted her face up to his. His orchestration was unnecessary. She wanted what was to come as much as he did.

"This is on my mind," he said and brushed his mouth over hers in a kiss that was light, nonthreatening—and as lethal as a nuclear bomb.

Ground zero seemed to be Roxy's brain. Her remaining reluctance and, it seemed, her bones, melted.

Unaware of the level of destruction, Nate feathered more kisses across her mouth until Roxy was breathless.

It had been so long since a man had made her feel desirable. They said sweet things, praising her beauty, her business sense, but the compliments were nothing but words—empty words. Nate, on the other hand, praised her with his touch, with the passion that flared in his storm-colored eyes when he looked at her.

Thoroughly seduced by the combination, Roxy kissed him back, letting him know she desired him as much as he wanted her.

Nate felt the moment when her resistance dissolved and waited for the elation of winning to swell his ego. He'd broken through her defenses, lured her into his arms and now she was melting there, waiting for him to do whatever he pleased.

He was a bit surprised that what he wanted to do was simply keep on kissing her. At least for now. Very soon that wouldn't be enough, but for now it was plenty. It allowed him to savor the taste of her, to inhale the womanly scent of her. It filled his head, flooded his senses. Her lips were not only willing, they were eager, passionate, demanding and loving.

Loving.

It was exactly how he wanted her. Pliant, and his alone. Funny, he'd never felt this protective of a woman before. Of course, none of the women that littered his past had been even a tenth as alluring as Roxy. She was not only beautiful, she wanted him for who he was, not for what he had made of himself or how much he was worth. She was self-sufficient, a successful businesswoman, and he suddenly wished that there was something he could give her that she couldn't give herself.

And so he kissed her more deeply, giving her the gift of passion because...

Because...

Damn! He really was in love with her! When had that happened? Nate wondered. Oh, sure, he'd played with the idea—a lot, actually—but he hadn't believed wholeheartedly in it.

Until now.

It felt good to admit he was irrevocably in love with Roxy, if only to himself. He would keep it to himself, too, get used to the idea before blurting it out. The concept of being so totally in love was strange and yet welcome. He'd known it would happen one day. Was glad it hadn't happened until Roxy had walked into his life.

One thing was certain. He wasn't letting her go. And this time, the decision had nothing to do with business or sex.

Well, not with business, at any rate. Nate kissed her more deeply, determined to win Roxy, heart and soul.

"You are so lovely," he murmured, brushing back the flying wisps of her hair.

The smile she gave him was shy, pleased, glowing. "I'm glad you think so," she whispered.

"You're a terrible liar, though," Nate said. "Was there even one bit of the game you enjoyed or understood tonight?"

Roxy's lashes dipped. She traced the curve of his chin,

her touch tentative and curious. "One," she admitted. "When the clock ran out and the game was over."

He settled her more comfortably in his arms. "Tonight," Nate said, "that was my favorite part of the game, too."

"Really?" She sounded doubtful.

"Really."

Her grin was beautiful. It lit her eyes, her whole face. "I'm glad," she said.

Nate squeezed her tighter, loath to let her go. "You know, I could get addicted to moments like these."

"Me, too," Roxy whispered. "Why don't you kiss me again?"

"If I do, I might not be able to stop."

"I wouldn't mind."

He'd thought the feeling was indigestion before, or something akin to it. Now Nate recognized the sensation for what it was. His heart had swelled with pleasure, with tenderness. "I want to make love to you, Rox," he said. "But as delightful as the surroundings are here, I think I'd prefer to do so in a bed."

Her lashes dipped again, sheltering him from a glimpse of her thoughts. They were mirrored so well in her eyes. Eyes so green, so soft, he knew contentment could be found by losing himself in them.

She'd been fighting back emotion all evening. Now it washed over her, sending her reeling. She loved him. The knowledge came unbidden, unwanted, and undisputed. She'd been so tangled up in the belief that her attraction to him was purely physical. Now that they were being a lot more physical, Roxy knew what she felt for Nate surpassed mere mating.

His hands slipped inside her coat, stroked along her spine, molding her tightly against him. His mouth angled over hers again; his tongue swept lightly along her bottom lip, met her tongue and tangled with it.

Mating, as Mother Nature had intended, began to take precedence over emotion in Roxy's mind. She dropped her arms from around Nate's neck and let her coat slip to the floor.

"Roxy," he murmured hoarsely. "There isn't—"

"The sofa," she purred, her lips brushing his once more, loath to end their kiss. "It unfolds."

"It what?" He looked down at her as if afraid he had heard wrong.

"It converts into a bed," Roxy said. "I used it when I was getting started and worked late. Now we use it if someone feels ill. It's just a single, but—"

He didn't let her finish. This time there was no doubting his desire for her. He'd been holding back, she realized. She was awfully glad he wasn't anymore.

Without breaking their kiss, Nate ripped his own coat off and flung it blindly into the corner.

"We should go slow," Roxy said, gulping a bit for air. Searching within herself for her lost equilibrium. If he hadn't been holding her, she was sure she would have collapsed. She felt dizzy just being near him.

"Yeah, we should," Nate agreed and shed another layer, tugging his sweater over his head, tousling his fair hair even more.

She'd thought him glorious that first day at the Pruitts', outfitted as he'd been in his tailor-made suit. She'd thought him gorgeous in his sweater and jeans. Roxy's fingertips brushed along the breadth of Nate's chest, enjoying the warmth of his skin through the fabric of his dark blue T-shirt. The cotton conformed to each muscled contour of his torso. He was absolutely awesome.

Nate made a sound deep in his throat, one of pure animal pleasure as her hand moved lower. He caught it, halting her exploration. "That's not what I call going slow," he chided. There was a wild, devil-may-care glint in his eyes, a roguish grin curving his lips.

"It isn't?" Roxy asked with false innocence.

"But then, neither is this," he said and skimmed her own sweater over her head. "Should we stop?"

Since he followed the question by nibbling on her earlobe, Roxy knew she wouldn't have called a halt to the delightful proceedings, even if she'd possessed a modicum of common sense. She kissed the rough, angled line of his jaw, followed it back to his mouth. His lips caught hers, crushed them in a caress that left her in no doubt about his ardor. Standing on tiptoe, the better to reach him, Roxy slipped her hands around Nate's neck and gave herself up to the rising pleasure.

When they drew apart, Roxy wished she could keep time totally at bay. There was not enough time to learn all she wanted to know about him. Not enough hours left that night in which to experience the joy of being in his arms, of having his lips meld with hers, to let their spirits soar in total accord.

"I haven't done this in a while," Roxy said.

The news was music to Nate's ears. The thought of another man making love with her was enough to put his teeth on edge.

"Truthfully, neither have I," he said.

It had been a while. While beautiful women had been plentiful in his life, those avaricious glints in their eyes worked on his libido about the same as a lapful of ice cubes. He was having no trouble in the fervor department now. Everything about Roxy stoked his furnace.

"Let's hope it's like riding a bicycle," he murmured. "If I recall correctly, this probably comes next." Nate slid his hand up over her ribs until he cupped the fullness of her breast. The silk texture of her blouse was cool, smooth, and a poor barrier against his exploration. Beneath the fabric he felt the coarser weave of her lacy bra and the lush weight of her in his palm. When he brushed his thumb over the budding crest, she turned to quicksilver in his arms.

Small explosions of desire went off in Roxy's brain. No other man's touch had elicited a tenth of the tumult of desire she felt with Nate.

"It does seem right," Roxy agreed a bit breathlessly. She leaned into him, going up on her toes again to close the distance between them, trailing tender, butterfly-light kisses on his eyes, his cheekbones, his nose. Curving one arm around his neck, she instigated another openmouthed kiss.

Nate's hands slipped down to cup her derriere, bringing them more intimately together as he deepened their kiss. His thoughts were incoherient. Pictures flashed in his mind, the fantasies he'd entertained about her. How tame they appeared next to the reality of the moment.

"The first time I saw you, I wanted to make love to you," he said.

"I'm glad," she purred and slipped away from his arms, one hand trailing down his arm until she held his hand. "Why don't you do so now?"

The narrow little couch was covered with toss pillows in various hues and designs. Together they cleared it. He stopped to kiss her again before folding the cushion out to create a far-too-narrow-but-quite-welcome foam mattress.

They barely got the bed fully opened before they sprawled on it, eager to be in each other's arms once more. Nate pushed off his shoes, fumbled briefly with the

buttons of her blouse. Then it was open, allowing his eyes
to feast on her gentle curves. He cupped her breast, lifted
her free of the lacy bra.

"Mmm. Perfect," he said softly.

Roxy's fingers brushed gently through his hair. "I'm
glad you like them."

How could he not? Her skin glowed warmly in the
meager light of the security lamps. The next time he made
love to her, Nate promised himself, it would be in full
light. Only then could he completely savor the sight of
every inch of her. For now he would rely on his other
senses. On touching the cool, satiny texture of her skin.
On tasting the welling bud of her breast. He bent, damp-
ening the pink tip with his tongue, lathing it, enjoying the
swell of desire that naturally lifted her body toward his.

Roxy shivered with delight.

"You're cold," Nate said.

"No. Never," she insisted and pulled him back to her
lips, needing to lose herself in his kiss. "I want you, Nate
Carrington," Roxy said. "I want you so much."

"And I you, Roxanne," he whispered.

Above them a galaxy of ornaments reflected glittering
flashes of light, suspended on invisible wires in the office
sky. Like planets, they twirled a bit in the warm currents
that wafted from the heating vents. Like the constellations
of the ancients, they looked down on the lovers and approved.

It was a long time before either Nate or Roxy managed
to utter a coherent word. They'd caressed, explored and
savored every touch, every kiss. And yet, as they lay replete and drowsy in each other's arms, Roxy congratu-
lated herself on holding back the words she had longed

to utter, and Nate wondered if he should have told her that he felt more than mere desire for her.

Finally they rose to get dressed. Roxy picked a bit of lint from Nate's sweater; he combed back her tumbling curls with his fingers. A last kiss was rehearsed at the main door of the shop before Roxy unlocked it. It was improved upon after she reset the alarm. Was delivered with a thoroughness that should have melted the snow beneath their feet in the parking lot.

Roxy brushed Nate's golden hair back from his temple, her touch tender. She wasn't sure yet if the circle of his arms was the place she wished to seek her "happily ever after," but it was certainly where she wanted to be that night.

"You going to the Pruitts' tomorrow evening?" Nate asked, his voice alone sending fresh chills of desire rushing along her spine.

She rested her head against his chest where she could hear and feel the strong, steady beat of his heart despite the thickness of his coat. "You think Wally will have made a decision by then?"

"Frankly," Nate said, "I don't much care at the moment. You want to go together?"

Roxy tilted her head back, looking at him. The mattress may well have been narrow, but they fit together on it perfectly. Had fit together perfectly, period. She hadn't felt this relaxed and happy in a long time. Maybe ever.

"You and me?" she asked.

Nate kissed the tip of her nose. "Don't act so surprised, Rox. If you recall, parking is a bitch in that neighborhood."

Roxy snuggled nearer him, enjoying the warmth of his body, the warmth in his eyes. If this was to be her only truly happy moment on earth, she was going to enjoy it to the hilt. She had no way of knowing if the emotion that welled in her soul was returned. In the event that she was in love—and in love alone—she would gather memories to horde away and savor once he forgot her.

"Parking? Is that the only reason you're asking?" she demanded.

"No," Nate admitted. "But I'm thinking of borrowing Casey's car again before I pick you up." His fingers stroked sensuously along her throat.

"Casey's? Why?" she asked, her words feathering against his mouth.

Nate's lips curved in a rakish grin a moment before he gave in to the need to kiss her again. "It's got a back seat," he said.

The Outlet sales receipts were totally forgotten. They stayed right where they were on Roxy's desk. When Nate offered once more to follow her home, to make sure she got there safely, she agreed to let him. The offer, and the sight of his headlights in her rearview mirror, gave her a warm, wonderful, cherished feeling. The sensation remained with her even after she was inside the house and he'd driven away. It stayed with her as she soaked in a bubble bath, as she slipped between the cool sheets of her bed. The first thought she had the next morning was that she would see him that evening.

The second was the realization that she was almost late for work.

Nate, on the other hand, was unable to sleep. He'd tossed and turned, and sworn every time he looked at the clock and found the hands creeping rather than rushing toward morning. There were just too many hours to fill until he could touch Roxy, hear her voice.

Around 3:00 a.m. he'd given up, gotten dressed, and

gone into the office. The place was eerie at that hour of the morning, but work was a sure cure to get a woman off a man's mind. He needed to shelve thoughts of Roxy. Needed space, time and distance. Even though he'd wanted his relationship with her to be an intimate one, the leap they'd taken in gaining that intimacy the evening before had left him numb.

Or was it the idea of being in love with her that had KO'd him? Love meant more than just getting a woman in bed. It meant sharing a home, a future, a life. They had all been nebulous things to him until now. He wanted Roxy to be part of his life. He'd made that decision days ago. Then he'd been thinking casual—a friendship based on physical attraction and business respect. That was no longer enough.

But he didn't want to think beyond that. Not quite yet, anyway. There was plenty to keep his mind off Roxy. Besides the regular day-to-day stuff, there was the remainders shop to plan, the company credit card to look into. More than enough to keep Roxy from stealing into his thoughts.

Or there was until he caught sight of the order form for her Midas Touch project lying dead center on his desk.

At The North Pole Outlet, Roxy fared about the same. In her absence, Bridget had put together a quick display in the gazebo area, integrating the expensive constellation ornaments the Triple C had delivered with their collection of metallic suns, moons and stars. The sight of them brought Nate all too vividly to mind, not to mention the time she had spent with him the evening before. The memory left her feeling warm, contented. Happy.

"Phone for you, Roxy," the woman at the register sang out. "It's Bridget and she sounds terrible."

She did indeed, Roxy agreed upon hearing Bridget's croaked greeting. "Don't tell me," Roxy urged. "You've got the flu."

"Great timing, huh?" Bridget said, her voice sounding weary and miserable. "Maybe if I dose myself with vitamin C and chicken soup, I can be half human by tonight to help you at The Midas Touch."

It was admirable to have such a die-hard employee. "Forget it," Roxy said. "Stay in bed and get all the way human so you can come back to the shop sooner. We've still got two weeks till Christmas and you know what a madhouse the place will be until then. I'll do The Midas Touch myself."

"You shouldn't. Take one of the other girls. Erica or Prudence or—"

"Don't be ridiculous," Roxy insisted. "I used to do all the trees in the shop by myself. I can handle this one alone."

"It's not that," Bridget said. "It's the idea of your working alone at night. It's not safe."

"I'll be fine."

"At least tell Nate you're going to be there without me," Bridget urged.

"Nate!" Roxy cried. "Why should I do that? This has nothing to do with him."

"Yeah, right," Bridget said, unconvinced. "Just tell him."

"I am not—"

"Roxy? Tell him."

Roxy sighed deeply. "It's really depressing to have such pushy employees."

"If you don't let him know, I'm going to get out of this deathbed and be there," Bridget threatened.

Roxy was sure her head of staff had made her voice

sound extra hoarse just to make her feel bad. "Okay, okay," she grumbled, capitulating. "I'll tell him."

"Thank you," Bridget said weakly.

"You'd better get well really quick," Roxy ordered and hung up the phone.

Great. What was she to do now? Despite the assurance she'd given Bridget that she could handle The Midas Touch tree on her own, Roxy wasn't looking forward to doing so. It would take four times as long since she would have to run up and down the ladders from one side of the tree to the other just to string the lights, let alone trying to carry the boxes of ornaments closer to the top branches. Perhaps she'd jumped the gun in trying to line up clients this year rather than wait until the next season.

"Bridget won't be in," Roxy told the woman at the register. "She's got the flu."

"Eww," the staffer moaned, screwing up her face in distaste. "I hope that doesn't mean we'll all end up passing it around."

Roxy hoped they didn't either, but doubted they would be lucky enough to totally avoid the nasty germ. She made a mental note to stock the refrigerator in the break room with gallons of orange juice and the first-aid kit with a giant-size container of pain relievers. Then she headed for the relative privacy of her office to call Nate.

9

At that very moment, Nate was barreling down the interstate, one hand on the wheel, the other wrapped around the mini cassette recorder he'd received on his last birthday. Back then, Ava had added sternly-voiced instructions for him to make frequent use of it. He only hoped the batteries were still going strong since that had been eight months ago and he hadn't remembered the recorder's existence, or Ava's orders, until now.

"Make a note to look into cellular phones, Ava darling," he dictated. "One for the Corvette and one for yourself. I think we're going to need them while we put this shop thing together. We'll both be on the road a good deal between the Triple C and TC Junior." Giving the as-yet-unborn shop a nickname made it seem more than just an idea. It was a goal now—one he had no intention of abandoning until it reached the fruition of an opening-day ribbon-cutting ceremony. He hoped Roxy would be at his side that day. Intended to make sure she was.

Once he'd begun thinking about the clearance shop, ideas had come hard and fast. He'd given up writing them down, resorting to the tiny tape recorder to document them. However, it hadn't *really* been the business he'd had in mind on that last note. He had a hankering to call

Roxy and there wasn't a convenient exit with a public phone anywhere in sight.

He had some questions to ask her about inventory control, about cash registers, about alarm systems, about...

Hell, he just wanted to hear her voice. There were just too many hours yet in the day before he was due to pick her up. She'd been on his mind constantly since they'd said good-night. He'd personally picked her stock selections for the restaurant job and loaded them into one of the small delivery vans—one with a heater that worked. Since the regular truck drivers were off on Sunday, he would be driving the vehicle himself. Real personalized service. Delivery with a smile and a kiss.

Especially the kiss.

Would she let him stick around the café tonight or eject him from the building, preferring not to mix business with pleasure? He sure hoped he merited a note in the pleasure column. She certainly headed his personal pleasure list.

"Contact our packing-box people and see if they also handle bags," Nate said into the recorder. "Three different sizes, I think, plus shopping bags. We want customers to be able to tote large quantities out of the place."

Was he being optimistic to envision customers with multiple shopping bags leaving TC Junior? Was he being foolish in driving all this distance to the outlet mall to look at leasable space already? Was he out of his mind to be thinking about a joint venture with Roxy—one that had absolutely nothing to do with business and was long-term? Incredibly long-term. Like a lifetime.

Hell, he'd only known her a week. But what a week! They had made love, spontaneously, fantastically—and in her shop! In retrospect, it sounded rather kinky, but Nate doubted there could have been a more perfect place to put their relationship on this wondrous new level than at The

North Pole Outlet. They'd been surrounded by the things she loved best, and many of them had been pieces he himself had especially chosen for his catalog. Surely it had been Kismet that they had consummated their budding intimacy among the trappings of Christmas. And extremely good sense on Roxy's part to put a fold-out bed in her office. Maybe he should think of putting one in his own office.

Maybe he should simply do something that would guarantee Roxy was always in whatever bed he was near.

Imagine *him* considering—scaring himself to death with the idea of—commitment.

His mother would be ecstatic. Or so he hoped.

His sister would be speechless. Yeah, right.

His father would be proud. Prouder that his son was settling down than he had ever been over Nate's business staying in the black. His old man had had doubts about the catalog ever being a success, but he'd never ceased to believe in, and lobby for, the benefits a man gained from having a loving wife.

A wife.

The word still had the power to make Nate feel as if someone were pouring concrete into his shoes. But when he thought about life without Roxy, he felt empty. He had never felt this way about another woman. He was glad he never had.

Thinking about a future with Roxy was fine. Deciding whether he should actually pop the question or not was something that definitely needed to be put off. Which was why he was putting all his attention on the clearance shop. Experience told him it would take months before the doors of TC Junior could open, but the sooner he had the groundwork done, the faster they could move. If they scheduled a midsummer opening date, the big fall catalog could go to print, advertising the new retail outlet. Coupons for ten-percent off could be included, labeled for in-shop use only. Should the merchandise be tagged to denote which season's catalog it last appeared in? What kind of reduction in price per piece could he take and still cover operating costs?

The Corvette streaked by a highway sign. It was half a mile to the next exit.

He had to take into consideration space rental, utilities, staffing.

Nate was nearly past the board before the legend painted on it clicked in his brain. At this exit could be found gas, food, lodging, rest rooms and...

Telephones.

All thoughts of Carrington's Christmas Clearance vanished from Nate's mind. He had to call Roxy. Needed to tell her that he cared.

"I'm so glad you called," Roxy said in relief. "I've been trying to get hold of you. I need to tell you something."

Ah, she did feel the same as he did, Nate thought joyously. He wasn't alone in this bewitchment. It was two-sided. They'd both been infected, both been bitten. They were both in—

"Bad news, I'm afraid," Roxy continued.

Shot down before he'd said a word. Nate could see his half-conceived dreams spiraling earthward in flames. He should have known better. It was too soon. It was— Hell, he wasn't going to let her dump him. She wanted him. She'd proved it quite satisfactorily the night before. All he needed to do was...was...well, *something,* and she would fall head over heels in love with him and then—

"Since Bridget has the flu, I'm stuck decorating the

tree alone tonight. That means I have to start work on it hours earlier than originally planned,'' Roxy said. ''I've already talked to the restaurant....''

It wasn't him. Thank God, it wasn't him she was rejecting. She was just doing what he'd been trying to do since they'd parted—she was putting her business first.

He understood that. He did it himself. Business always came first. Neither of them would have gotten where they were without adhering to that steadfast rule. It was an unshakable truth, a way of life, a religion.

Damn, but he hated that rule.

''Will there be any problem getting the materials to the restaurant earlier?'' Roxy asked.

''Not a bit,'' Nate assured her. ''I'm the one driving the van. What do you say to me leaving it at your place, we take your car to the Pruitts', then come back and—''

''I'm not going to the Pruitts' tonight,'' she said. ''I put them off. Asked if dinner could be bumped back a night. At least for me. You go on ahead.''

He wasn't about to go anywhere without her.

His words should be music to her ears, Roxy told herself. Nate was talking business, talking accommodation to her needs, not something a small retailer—which she most definitely was—could expect to receive from a wholesaler. She was blessed that Carrington's Christmas Catalog—well, okay, Nate himself—was willing to go the extra mile. Deliver at an extreme hour. Provide what she needed most at the drop of the proverbial hat.

Boy, had he ever provided what she needed most the night before!

So why did she feel depressed over the whole business? Why did she want him to say, *To hell with the restaurant! Let's spend the evening together. Let's get to know each other better.*

Let's make love.

Nate wasn't going to say it. It was ridiculous for her to long for it. She barely knew the man. Oh, sure, she knew *of* him, but the Carrington who ran the million-dollar catalog business and the Nate who turned her knees to mush and clouded her mind to everything but him were two different people. Weren't they?

If she had to make a choice between them, which Nate would she choose? Her business couldn't do without the goodwill of the Triple C. Despite the fact that Nate thought she didn't buy enough stock from him, Roxy considered his company her major supplier. He might only have a quarter of her business, but the other three-quarters was shared by ten different companies. She should choose Nate the businessman. Her profit margin was at stake.

But her heart didn't care two hoots about the profit margin. It was more inclined to rate kisses far above such mundane things as prompt delivery and discounts for even prompter payment of invoices.

"What a minute," Nate said on the phone. "Did you say you were decorating the restaurant tree by yourself?"

"Have to," Roxy answered. "If you heard how bad Bridget sounds—"

"And there's no one else to help?"

"Not if I want to keep the store fully staffed. As it is, I have to lock up at nine tonight because—"

"You do?" he interrupted, his voice flat.

"Not to worry. I'll be at the restaurant before you come by," Roxy assured him. "I'll help you unload and you can be on your way to Wally's within minutes."

"To hell with that," Nate said. "I'll pick you up. You are not going to decorate that monster tree all by yourself tonight."

And here she'd been thinking it was nice to have a man feeling protective of her. What had she been thinking?

"I'm not an empty-headed doll, Nate. I'm perfectly capable of—"

"Whoa, slow down, sugar," he insisted. "I didn't say you weren't capable."

"Yes, you did," Roxy countered. "You said—"

"I said," Nate declared a bit more loudly in an effort to override her rising anger, "you weren't going to do it by yourself. I'll help. I'll be there."

Roxy wasn't sure she'd heard him correctly. "You'll be there? Why?"

She thought it sounded as though he took a deep breath before answering.

Nate made his announcement so quietly, the background sound of traffic behind him nearly drowned out the words. "I'll be there because you need me to be there."

No sweeter words had ever been uttered, but Roxy was positive that she hadn't heard right. She'd been hoping he would fall in love with her; wishing it would come to pass. Well, he hadn't said the magic word, but her imagination could fill in the blanks, turning words she had heard into ones she longed to hear.

Roxy stared at the phone receiver a moment, then took a chance. "I really do need you there. Thank you," she said softly.

"You're welcome," Nate said.

Walter Pruitt strolled into the homey kitchen. The scent of beef cooking in a medley of spices filled the air. So did the sounds of the holidays. In the background the radio was playing one of Goldy's favorite songs. She sang along, putting a lot of feeling into her rendition. "Santa," the recorded singers and Goldy pleaded sweetly in sync, "make me his bride for Christmas."

"You can stop your chopping," Wally said.

Goldy stopped only her singing. She glanced up from dicing apples for her strudel and grinned happily. "So Nate canceled out on us, too? Excellent."

Wally dropped into the chair opposite her. "You've been working for two days getting ready for this dinner and now you're happy that neither Roxy nor Nate can make it tonight? All these years we've been together and there are still times when I don't understand you."

"You aren't supposed to," Goldy said. "It would take the mystery out of our marriage. Besides, everything I've made thus far can handle being stuck in the fridge another day. In fact, since we're having pot roast, and I've been cooking it at a low temperature, it will be even tastier tomorrow. Tonight you can take me out to dinner."

"I can, huh?"

Goldy put her knife down and folded her arms on the table. "All this matchmaking makes me in the mood for a little romance myself, Pruitt. What can you offer me?"

"How about Southern-fried chicken takeout? I think we got a coupon in the mail for three dollars off."

"You certainly know how to sweep a girl off her feet," Goldy said ruefully. "I hope that large package with my name on it that you lugged in here and put under the tree isn't a snowblower."

Wally tried not to look guilty. "Well, if it is, you know we need a new one." Mentally he made a note to do more shopping. This time he figured it would be safer to do it away from the hardware department.

"So what did Nate say?" Goldy demanded. "What excuse did he give for avoiding us this evening?"

"He said he was helping Roxy decorate a tree."

"Oh, this is better than I had hoped," Goldy declared. "It calls for a celebration. Put on your Sunday best, sweetheart. We're going out and, frankly, a box of fried chicken doesn't suit my mood in the least."

"It doesn't?" Wally bleated unhappily. "I still don't understand why you're so chipper."

Goldy gathered up the cut apples, scooping them off the cutting board and into a bowl. "Because Nate and Roxy will be together tonight, of course," she said as she sprinkled the fruit with lemon juice.

"We're not talking Cayman Islands togetherness," Wally said. "They're just trimming a tree for some business or other. That hardly seems like a romantic activity. It sounds more like they work awfully strange hours."

"But don't you see?" Goldy pressed. "For them business is everything. That they are working together, and will probably still be doing so at the bewitching hour, is how it should be. I do hope they invite us to the wedding."

Wally snorted. "Wedding? How do you get from tree trimming to wedding invitations?"

His wife gave him a look that told him she was more aware of these things than he was. He'd seen it a lot over the years. Damned if she hadn't been right more times out of mind, too.

"Besides," he reminded her, "we'll be out of here on Christmas Day. We won't be around to get an invitation even if they send one. We'll be in Maui, which is where we'd be right now if you didn't insist on spending the holiday in a cold climate."

"I do it for you, dear," Goldy said, stretching plastic wrap over the bowl of sliced apples. "We tried Christmas in the Islands once. You looked ridiculous as a Santa in scarlet shorts. You haven't the legs for it." She paused before the refrigerator, one hand resting thoughtfully against her cheek. "Either the Caymans or Hawaii would be wonderful places for a honeymoon at this time of year. Why don't we get out the pictures of our trips when Nate and Roxy are here tomorrow night? They are such busy people, they need help when it comes to arranging their private life."

"They do, do they?" Wally murmured. "I thought you kept busy enough arranging my private life."

Goldy grinned. "I only practice on you, dear one. Do you know, I think we should try that new French restaurant tonight."

When Wally made a face at the idea, she took pity on him. "You'll like it. We've got a coupon to use for ten dollars off on one entrée."

Wally brightened immediately.

He wasn't doing badly for a guy who'd been awake for nearly forty hours, Nate thought as he pulled into the driveway at Roxy's home. It had been a mistake to stand in the shower as long as he had, but the hot water had felt too good to step out of it quickly. The steam had made him feel drowsy and his bed had looked awfully welcoming despite the tangled sheets. However, Roxy was waiting for him. Roxy needed him. He could make it. He *would* make it. They were due at The Midas Touch at ten. The tree there was ten feet tall, so by the time they got finished stringing a thousand or more lights and hanging a couple of gross of ornaments, he only needed to be awake for, say, another six or seven hours.

Oh, God. He would never make it.

He should have taken a nap. Should not have driven the hour out to the outlet mall; should not have spent quite so much time with the very accommodating realty agent who'd hotfooted it over with the keys to the empty 10,000-square-foot storefront.

He hadn't felt the least bit sleepy as he'd roamed the echoing space. The adrenaline was pumping and his mind was going a mile a minute. He'd had to turn the tape in the recorder over, he'd dictated so many thoughts into it.

The place was perfect. The location was extremely visible, parking was convenient and the lease price was next to ridiculous it was so low. He wanted to see what Roxy thought first before taking it. And probably Ava, since he would be turning Junior over to her care. Roxy's word would hold more weight since she had the necessary retail background and experience. She was definitely the one to consult. He thought she would agree with him, though.

And if she didn't? Well, he was sure she would give him very definite, logical reasons why she advised against the location. They could look for a different place together.

Would Roxy be as enthusiastic as he was over the new venture? Nate hoped so. Daydreams where they discussed sales promotions, merchandise pricing, even staff management—in the intimate comfort of a bed, naturally—had entertained him throughout the long drive back to town. They danced in his head still, like frantically frugging sugarplums, the bed taking precedence. What were sugarplums, anyway? his overtired mind wondered. Did they look anything like the handblown, gold-tinged, glitter-dusted, fruit-shaped ornaments that filled a good part of the delivery van he was driving?

The van lacked a lot when it came to making an impressive arrival. His Corvette was jaw-droppingly awesome, after all. But the women who'd gotten hot over his car had never stayed in his life for long. Nate had a feeling Roxy would find the delivery truck far more impressive,

not because it had Carrington's Christmas Catalog emblazoned in large green letters along the side, but because it
was loaded with the merchandise she'd requested.

She was a woman in a million. One of a kind.

She had been watching for him. He'd barely turned the
engine off when she slipped out the front door, pausing
only long enough to lock the house behind her.

Nate glanced at the dashboard clock. It was barely nine-
thirty. At this rate, they would get to The Midas Touch
fifteen minutes early. Maybe he could slow her down. He
could think of quite a lot of pleasant ways to do so.

Roxy looked lovely surrounded by the light of the hun-
dred-plus pixie-size lights in the shrubbery. She'd worn
her hair down so that it spilled in tumbling waves over
the shoulders of her light-colored coat. Nate wanted nothing more than to gather her close, bury his face in those
russet waves and inhale her precious scent. He got out of
the van with that very intention foremost in his mind.

"Hi," she greeted, her breath turning to vapor in the
cold air.

"Hi," he said, and moved closer, intent on claiming a
kiss.

Roxy took a couple of fancy steps, skipping blithely
away from him. "I brought some nourishment along."
She lifted an attractive bright red cloth shopping bag. A
felt evergreen had been stitched to the side of it, decorated
with odd bits of ribbon, sequins and buttons. Tiny presents
wrapped in gold lamé were scattered beneath the lower
branches. "It isn't much," Roxy said. "Just a thermos of
decaf coffee and a couple handfuls of fresh-baked cookies
Ava brought into the shop today."

Ava baked cookies? Since when?

"We must have great minds," Nate said. He raised the

not-so-attractive brown paper bag that held his own offering. "Black coffee and raspberry Danish."

"A veritable feast," Roxy agreed, beating him to the
van's passenger-side door. She yanked it open and hopped
inside.

There were times when self-sufficient, independent
women could really get on a man's nerves. Here he was,
anxious to prove his worth through little acts of courtesy,
and she made even the appearance of an effort impossible
to perform.

"So," Roxy said as he got behind the wheel, snapped
his seat belt in place and started the engine once more,
"do you think Wally will choose you or me tomorrow
night?"

Business. She always went back to business. He was
savvy enough to catch subtle nuances, though, Nate told
himself, rebooting his stalled ego. This time Roxy was
using business as a blind to escape what was really on her
mind.

"So what exactly about last night are you regretting?"
he asked.

Her eyes flew to his. "Nothing," she claimed as he
backed out onto the street.

She was doing some major dissembling. "It has to be
something. I can practically feel a ten foot pole poking
me in the chest, insuring that I keep my distance," Nate
said.

"Don't be ridiculous," Roxy said. "Remember, I told
you I loved what we did last night."

"And did so very politely," Nate agreed. "Your
mother would be proud."

"There's no reason to be sarcastic," Roxy insisted. "I
thought it was what you wanted to hear."

"So you don't really care about me," he said flatly.

"I barely know you."

"I barely know you and it doesn't matter a cat's a—"

"Pull over here," Roxy insisted sternly.

He'd done it now. If she'd been the one driving, she would have kicked him out of her car. As it was, he foresaw being barred from helping at The Midas Touch. Nate pulled over, fully expecting Roxy to yank the door open and hoof it back to where they'd left her car in the driveway barely a block away.

She didn't get out of the van. "Listen," she said, turning to face him. "It doesn't matter that I don't know that much about you. I know enough to feel the way I feel. I do care about you. More than I ever believed possible. But that's not the crux here, Nate. Wally Pruitt has been stringing us both along for nearly a week now. To do so is ridiculous. For him, because this is the season when he usually works and he's deliberately keeping himself out of work. For us, because we could find someone else to do the same jobs we've been offering him, and probably for less money, too."

Bless her little P&L-inked heart. Nate went nose to nose with her. "What if I said I was waiving the minimum-time-employed stipulation on the Triple C's health plan for him?"

Roxy twisted more in her seat, leaned closer to him. "I'd say you're bringing up the big guns. Perhaps he'd prefer three weeks' paid vacation."

"Or four," Nate countered.

"Profit sharing," Roxy said.

"Stock option."

"You aren't on the stock market," she reminded him.

"I could be," Nate warned, then offered a compromise. "We could also share Wally." If it gave him an edge in winning her heart and soul, then, damn it, he would hire the jolly old procrastinating soul whether he needed him or not.

"I'd get him for the holidays and the last two weeks of July?" Roxy asked.

"No problem."

"How would we work out salary and benefits?"

"Contract. Your lawyers can talk to my lawyers," Nate said. "We'll tie up every loose end, cover every eventuality."

Roxy studied his face a moment more. Her eyes dipped to his lips. "Done," she said softly.

Nate knew the script from here. He kissed her. Roxy sealed the deal with gratifying enthusiasm.

"So, do we repitch the job over dessert tomorrow night?" she asked when they parted.

Damn, but he loved her. The woman had the heart of a shark disguised in mermaid packaging. They were going to do tremendous things together.

"We could let Wally make the first move," Nate suggested. "*Or* we could run him into a box canyon and see how he reacts."

Roxy's smile widened. "I like the way you think, Carrington," she said.

"Ditto, Mercer," he murmured.

"We need to get him alone so Goldy isn't there to give him backup."

"I'm sure together we can arrange that," Nate said. "But at the moment, there's something else I'd like to discuss with you."

When he released the catch on his seat belt, Roxy followed suit and moved into his arms.

They were fifteen minutes late getting to The Midas Touch.

10

"Sorry we're late," Roxy said to the irritated maître d'
when they arrived at the restaurant. "My closer came
down with the flu so I had to unexpectedly lock up the
shop."

"And I was out of town and only just got back," Nate
claimed, taking a share of the blame on his broad shoulders. Roxy's heart swelled with pride at the action. He
really was someone special.

"I see," the maître d' said, his tone politely disapproving.

Probably hadn't forgiven her for introducing the Pruitts
to his establishment, Roxy figured. Well, while she would
most definitely return to redo their decor, she never intended to eat at The Midas Touch again.

She was glad the cold maître d' would be leaving soon.
According to her agreement with the restaurant's manager, she and Nate would be locked inside the building
until five in the morning when the cleaning crew arrived.
Had she mentioned that little detail to Nate? Roxy had a
feeling it had slipped her mind. And at the moment, he
was dealing with the stuffy help's attitude.

"Anxious to be off, are you?" Nate asked. "Then give
us a hand, won't you, chum?" He dumped the carton of
twinkle lights he'd been carrying into the man's arms.

"Ms. Mercer will tell you where to put this then you can join me at curbside to unload the rest."

Apparently such duties were beneath the maître d's dignity. He deposited the lights near the current tree with its meager selection of ornaments and disappeared into the kitchen. A moment later three waiters came out, eager to help. The maître d' didn't reappear until the van had been unloaded and ladders were set up on either side of the tree. Then he breezed by them on his way out the door, pausing only long enough to lock them inside the building.

The moment they were alone, Roxy began ripping boxes open, her enthusiasm and delight akin to that of a child on Christmas morning. "Oh, these are lovely, Nate!" she cried as she unearthed each of the ornaments. "But we can't put them up until we rescue that poor tree from its current dressing. We're going to take it from obscurity to four-star. Give it a rank higher than any gourmand would give the menu here. In the morning I want the staff so dazzled, they'll start to believe in Santa Claus again."

Already perched high above her on a ladder, Nate reached for the topmost ornament on the tree. "That's a tough order, considering you're dealing with a Scrooge of a maître d'. That guy's got the world's shortest memory where tips are concerned."

"Probably didn't recognize you in your working clothes," Roxy soothed. "Hey, how are you going to get down the ladder with your arms that full of ornaments?"

"I'm simply being efficient," Nate said. "You ever play catch?" The next moment he dropped a large ornament into her hands.

When at last the tree was stripped, Nate proposed a break. Roxy's steam was up, though. She wanted to get started creating magic. That was what decorating a tree always seemed to be to her. When it was done right—and she always tried to do it very right—there was a special glow that warmed her deep inside. She called it the Christmas spirit and thanked the heavens that she was in a business that let her savor the special feeling year-round.

"This is going to be great," she announced, picturing in her head how the tree would look when they were done.

"Absolutely," Nate said. He didn't sound as excited as she was. In fact, Roxy realized, he sounded dead tired.

He'd collapsed at the nearest table and was pouring a strong dose of coffee from his thermos using a cup from the servers' station. The departed Scrooge would not be pleased, but Roxy doubted Nate much cared.

She went to him, slid her arms around his neck from behind, rested her cheek against his fair hair. "You aren't coming down with something, are you?" she asked.

"I'm just a little tired," Nate said. "Let me get a hit or two of caffeine and I'll be fine again."

Roxy slipped onto his lap, studying his face at close range. His eyes were dull, his leer—when he tried it— weak. "You look like a man who hasn't slept in days."

"Nonsense," Nate declared. "It isn't that long ago since I caught a few winks. It just wasn't last night, that's all."

"You didn't sleep at all?" she pressed, concerned.

"I'll be fine," he said.

He wouldn't.

"You should have told me," Roxy insisted.

"Just did," Nate said. "I'll bet if you kiss me, I'd revive really fast."

Roxy smiled softly and stroked her fingers back through his hair. "I'll bet you would, but you'd still be useless when it came to decorating the tree. I don't want you falling off the ladder and getting hurt.''

''Not sure whether workmen's comp covers me?'' he asked.

''No! Besides, you'd probably break your neck and then where would I be?''

''Yeah,'' Nate agreed. ''It's a real pain stepping over a body while trying to get some work done. I'll be careful.''

''I said no,'' Roxy repeated more empathically. ''That means I'm not letting you even try to help. Understand?''

''Uh-huh,'' he murmured and nuzzled her throat. ''Sounds like you'd make a good mom.''

She wasn't so sure about that. ''I think that involves more than the ability to say no firmly.''

''All right, you'd be a good dog owner, then,'' Nate said. ''Do you want one?''

''A dog?''

''A kid. Children.''

She'd never thought about having any. Not seriously, anyway. Until Nate had come along, there had been little hope of her ever falling in love, much less becoming a parent. The only children she'd had any dealings with were her nieces and nephews and the tykes that came to see Santa in her store. Even within her family, her interaction with the younger set was usually incredibly brief ''I suppose I'd like to have children,'' Roxy admitted carefully.

''Me, too,'' Nate said. ''To have a really great Christmas, you need kids.''

He was right. He was half-asleep, but he was right Christmas was much more than just pretty decorations gaudy wrappings and unnecessary presents. It was a celebration of life, a renewal of hope. In the churches they told of a special Child's birth, and it was only in the faces of little children that the peace on earth He had preached could still be read.

Roxy trailed her fingers down over Nate's jaw, traced the fullness of his lower lip. "Would you like to join my family for dinner Christmas Day?" she asked.

"If you're willing to run the gauntlet of the Carrington family Christmas Eve," he said. "Actually, I'll go with you even if you forgo the circus on the 24th."

"I wouldn't miss it," Roxy said, and kissed him lingeringly. "Now, if you don't mind, I've got to get back to work. I want you to take a nap."

Nate stopped her from leaving, grabbing her hand before she could get away. "Rox."

"Yes?"

"I love you."

It was impossible not to kiss him again. "I love you, Nate," Roxy said quietly. "It feels great, doesn't it?"

He wasn't finished, though. "Marry me, Roxanne," he said. "Marry me and have my children. Marry me and make my life complete."

"Nate—"

He stilled her, laying his forefinger gently against her lips. "I don't know how I've managed to get this far without you, Rox. And I sure as hell can't imagine continuing on without you. Don't make me go it alone any longer."

More elegantly spoken words had never been uttered. He summed up what she had been feeling and hadn't been able to completely admit, even to herself.

Roxy took his hands in hers. Kept her eyes on the long, strong length of his fingers as they grasped hers tightly. "Nate, I—"

"It's too soon, isn't it?" he demanded. "Blame my ill timing on sleep deprivation. It's just that—"

Roxy kissed him to shut him up.

"Was that a yes?" he asked, long minutes later.

"It was a definite yes," she said. "I'd love to marry you, however—"

"I hate howevers."

Roxy wrinkled her nose at him but stayed secure in the circle of his arms. "Our businesses, Nate. I've worked hard to build the Outlet, to become the businesswoman I am. I'm proud of the shop and would hate to see it gobbled up by a giant like the Carrington Catalog. I love you very much, love the idea of being your wife, but to keep my shop separate, I'm almost willing to forgo marriage. We could, you know, simply live together."

"We could," he admitted. "In fact, we can."

"Don't sound so relieved," Roxy advised. "I said we could, not that I wanted to. I'm a dyed-in-the-wool traditionalist at heart. If we're going to have children—"

"We are if I have anything to do with it," Nate said. "And I plan to do that 'it' a lot."

"Then I'll see you at the altar, Mr. Carrington," Roxy said. "Although I don't know when to work it into my schedule. I haven't much experience in having a personal life, you see."

Nate hugged her tightly. "Tell me about it," he murmured. "Maybe we can learn how to have one together."

"Absolutely," Roxy agreed. "Any suggestions on how we start? After doing this tree, I've got the whole decorating program to put together and market, inventory to complete, the travel agency to buy out, the shop to enlarge and next holiday season to plan and buy for. Oh, and this thing with Wally Pruitt to finish. What about you?"

Nate was unsuccessful in hiding a yawn from her. "Sleep sounds awfully good," he admitted.

It did to her, too, especially since she would now spend the rest of her life sleeping next to him.

"Take a nap," she urged. "I'll wake you if I need you."

"Promise?"

"Promise," Roxy vowed and sealed it with a kiss that promised him a lifetime of love.

When the restaurant's cleaning staff arrived at 5:00 a.m., it was to find a glittering gold-trimmed tree and Roxy and Nate asleep together beneath its branches.

The scent of freshly baked cinnamon bread fought with the aroma of roasting meat while in the background a slightly scratchy-sounding record played on the stereo. Marigold Pruitt had dug out her favorite album and was humming along to her favorite song, "Christmas Bride."

She leaned back against Wally's massive chest, content to be in the circle of her husband's arms. "This brings back memories," she murmured.

"This does?" Wally asked, squeezing her fondly.

"Yes," Goldy said, "but I meant the song. I sang along with this record the entire holiday season the year I met you, I wanted to marry you so badly."

"And it worked," her husband said. "Santa must have thought you were a very good girl to deserve me."

Goldy chuckled softly. "He wasn't paying very close attention to what we were doing then."

"Could be, he was," Wally declared. "After all, there is good and there is *good*. I thought you were being awfully good to me."

"I was good *for* you," Goldy corrected, "just like Roxy is good for Nate and he is for her. In addition to their tree-trimming activities, I certainly hope they've been seeing more of each other since we all had lunch.''

Wally leaned closer to whisper in her ear. ''Define what you mean by 'more of each other,''' he said, a distinct twinkle in his eyes.

''Watch it, Pruitt,'' she cautioned, fondly patting the massive arm that encircled her waist. ''I'll tell the real Santa on you. If we were more experienced at being Cupid's agents, we would have had this dinner a couple of days ago to make sure they were thrown together.''

''Couldn't,'' Wally reminded her. ''I was otherwise booked and a dinner without me would have looked damn odd under the circumstances.''

Goldy sighed. ''Yes, you're right, but it also means that if my matchmaking efforts don't bear fruit, the disaster can be laid at your feet.''

With a theatrical groan, Wally released her and took a chair at the carefully set kitchen table. Arranging four place-settings around the gigantic bouquet Nate had sent earlier in the week had been a tricky business. Especially since Goldy had felt honor-bound to encircle it with pieces of fruit from Roxy's generous offering. ''You did what you could,'' Wally said.

''No, if I'm going to be truthful, the real credit goes to you, dear one,'' Goldy insisted. ''You were the one who held off giving them both a decision.''

''At your request.''

''But I know it wasn't something you enjoyed doing.''

''You were the one who made sure she knew about the flowers and the show tickets,'' Wally reminded.

Goldy nodded. ''Yes, and Roxanne reacted just as hoped she would. She, after all, was the toughest of the nuts to crack.''

''Speaking of nuts...'' Wally murmured.

His wife handed him a bowl of freshly cracked walnuts and went to check on her dinner again. "When she called earlier, Roxy said Nate was picking her up."

"Sounds encouraging," Wally agreed.

"But not good enough as far as I'm concerned. I want them to stay together once we're out of the picture. So we need something more," Goldy said. "Something truly romantic."

"Too bad we don't have a fireplace," he said. "The one we had that year in Maine made me feel in the mood for romance."

"You're always in the mood for what you think is romance," Goldy chided. "But I think you're on the right track. Unplug all the living-room lamps and light those scented candles the neighbors made for us last year."

With a long-suffering sigh, Wally pushed back to his feet. "Do we have to have them at the dinner table, too? I like to see my food as I eat."

"Party pooper," Goldy murmured under her breath. "Oh, all right. Light them only in the living room. Push the furniture back a bit while you're at it. And find some soft dance music."

"Yes, dear," he said. "And while I set the stage, what are you going to do?"

Goldy smiled widely before turning her attention once more to the pots on the stove. "Me? Oh, I think I'll just add a little something extra to the meal."

"Something extra? Like what?" he asked.

"Magic, dear," Goldy said. "Just a touch of Christmas magic."

"Sorry we're a day late," Roxy said as she and Nate stepped over the Pruitt threshold.

"We brought wine, though," Nate added. "Does that make us more welcome?"

Wally waved them both farther into the house. "You bet. But not to worry," he told them. "Dinner's running even later than you are."

The heavenly scent coming from the kitchen begged leave to differ. The tapers glowing about the room looked as if they had been lit for some time now. On the turntable, the last strands of a bossa nova rhythm were just fading away.

"Make yourselves at home," Wally urged, taking their coats. He stopped by the stereo system and reset the needle to the first song on the record. The lettering on the dog-eared album cover leaning against the speaker grill advertised that Frank Sinatra was the featured performer at the Pruitts' that night.

"Roxy! Nate!" Goldy greeted, giving them a group hug that effectively closed the space they'd carefully put between each other. "I'm afraid I got carried away shopping earlier and lost track of the time. Dinner will be ready in half an hour or less. Oh, you brought wine? Wally, why don't you get out the glasses. We can all sip while we're waiting. Perhaps dance a bit."

Five minutes later the Pruitts had retreated to the kitchen, ostensibly to put the finishing touches to the meal. Roxy and Nate were left alone in the dimly lit front room, thin-stemmed wine goblets in hand, listening to Old Blue Eyes croon about a girl from Ipanema.

Very unChristmas-like, Roxy thought. She had expected a man who looked like Santa Claus to be a Christmasaholic as she was. As she suspected Nate was.

Nate put his glass aside and took her hand. "Aren't we supposed to be dancing?"

"Dancing? When have you ever been at a business dinner where dancing was required?" Roxy asked.

"Every awards presentation or conference dinner I ever attended required dancing," Nate answered. "I think I'll enjoy it more since I'm dancing with you instead of a manufacturer's talkative wife."

Roxy went into his arms easily. "Are all manufacturers' wives chatty then?"

"Only the ones that show up at conference and awards dinners. Or so it has seemed to me most of the time. When you go with me, you'll be the exception," Nate said, cheek to cheek with her. He swayed with the music, barely moving his feet.

Roxy followed suit, more interested in his nearness than in actually dancing. "All this *atmosphere* makes me suspect it isn't job hunting but matchmaking that is in the air," she said.

"Should we tell them the match is already made?" Nate asked.

"No." Roxy tossed her head. "Let them stew for a bit."

Nate inhaled deeply, obviously enjoying the aroma that filled the house. "Smells more like pot roast to me," he announced. "Definitely pot roast. Now there's something you can't get at The Midas Touch. Think they'd add it to the menu if we suggested it?"

"I doubt it," Roxy murmured.

"Can you make it?" he asked.

Roxy smiled into his shoulder. "Cooking isn't one of my talents. How about you?"

"I've been known to turn steak into charcoal in the broiler," Nate said. "Not everyone can do that successfully, you know. Or so the fire department tells me."

"So I've heard. Looks like we could very well starve," Roxy said.

Nate nuzzled her hair. "How about if we call carry-out a lot? I've got a fast-dial gizmo on the phone and fast-food numbers already programmed in it."

"That's a very seductive offer," Roxy allowed.

"I could make an even better one," he offered. "What do you think about—"

"Oh!" Goldy Pruitt exclaimed happily, emerging from the kitchen. "This has always been one of my favorite songs. Wally, come dance with me."

Wally stuck his head out of the open doorway, a piece of celery in his hand. "Me dance?" he demanded. "Buttercup, I haven't done that in years. I don't think I remember how."

Nate and Roxy exchanged a quick look and separated.

"Then allow me, Goldy," Nate said smoothly.

"Oh, no. Nate, truly I didn't mean..." Goldy's voice trailed away as she cast a pleading glance to where her husband stood unmoving.

"Nonsense. My pleasure," Nate insisted and drew her into the center of the room.

While Nate had their hostess occupied, Roxy took her chance and bore down on their hapless host. Despite her diminutive size, Wally retreated before Roxy's determined rush. "I missed lunch today," she said. "Think I could steal a piece of celery, too? You know, to tide me over?"

"Ah, sure," Wally mumbled uneasily as he backed away.

Roxy waited to attack until they were far from the doorway and he was offering her the plate of fresh cut vegetables. "So what's the deal, Wally? Christmas is nearly here and *you*—" Roxy stabbed her own stalk of celery at him for emphasis ''—are still out of a job. Was the whole newspaper story a con job? Is that why you have been playing Nate and me against each other? At this late date you can't possibly be entertaining other job offers. There aren't many places in need of a Santa even at this time of year, much less year-round.''

''I—''

''What's the problem, Wally? What I've offered you is generous. What Nate's offered you is even more generous.''

''Well, I—''

''What is it you want?'' Roxy persisted. ''A company car? Nate could cough that up, I suppose, if you signed a contract. For that kind of perk, I think he'd need a guarantee that you could perform. And I don't mean playing a jolly Saint Nick.''

Literally wedged in the farthest corner of the room now, Wally no longer looked the part of Santa. Roxy doubted a personage with the true spirit of Christmas would have succumbed under her litany of questions.

''It's not that,'' Wally bleated. ''The truth is...''

Roxy folded her arms over her chest, donned a straight face and listened. It wasn't an easy demeanor to maintain. Especially the straight-face part.

Replete with pot roast and wine and Roxy at his side, Nate wasn't feeling too bad. Of course, sleeping most of the day away had been very beneficial. Although, with Roxy sharing his bed, sleep wasn't all he'd done.

It was late when they left the Pruitts, the explanations Roxy had browbeat Wally into giving and the much-delayed pot roast drawing the evening out longer than expected.

The next time he tried to hire a guy in a Santa suit,

Nate promised himself, he was going to make sure he checked out all the malls. As Roxy said, if either of them had managed to take the time to do some holiday shopping, they might well have stumbled onto the fact that Wally was suiting up every day in his Claus crimson at Bradshaw and Sons, the local independent upscale department store. Pruitt had never been interested in a full-time job. He and Goldy preferred the freedom of spending a good part of the year on a beach. It didn't matter whether the beach was in Florida, Hawaii or the Caymans. The Pruitts frequented all three. Travel, they claimed, was the benefit they most enjoyed after getting lucky with a couple of minor investments they'd made over twenty years before. "Who would have thought personal computers would become so popular?" Wally had asked.

"We would have told you Wally wasn't interested right away if we hadn't sensed there was something very special about both of you," Marigold had claimed. "But there is. We believe very strongly in fate—" Well, who wouldn't, having made a comfortable fortune with computer stocks? "But we also believe in giving fate a little help now and then."

Nate put his arm around Roxy's shoulders as they walked back to his parked car. "So you played bad cop, huh?" he asked.

Laughter burbled in her voice. "Oh, no. More like stern, slightly disappointed parent. I play it all the time with my employees when they think I've got too soft a heart to turn them off."

"I'll watch my step from here on in," Nate promised. "So what kind of beans did Wally spill? I only heard part of it since Goldy kept leading the conversation back to the joys of beach life."

"Maybe we should try one sometime and see if she's right," Roxy said.

"Like on a honeymoon?" he asked.

"Could be. If we could ever get away."

"You know," Nate said as he unlocked the car door. "One of my more successful suppliers once told me it was a poor company owner who never managed to arrange his own time off."

Roxy gathered the trailing skirt of her coat and slipped into the bucket seat. "Was that a comment on my managerial skills?"

"A hint, shall we say?" he suggested. "I not only want to spend the rest of my life with you, I'd like to see you now and again during that life."

"I'd like to see you more often, too," Roxy agreed. "I'll try to do better at planning time off. Now, get in the car and I'll regale you with highlights from Wally's confession."

Nate was behind the wheel quickly. "All right. Give," he ordered once they were rolling. "Were we being taken for a ride by Wally and spouse?"

"Yes," Roxy said. "But they weren't doing it to see how much they could get out of us. Which reminds me— would you like to attend the ballet?"

"You got them *Nutcracker* tickets?" Nate sounded flabbergasted. "Damn."

"Is that your opinion of the ballet?" Roxy pressed. "Or just a generalized bit of frustration?"

"Pretty generalized," he admitted. "The ballet can't hold a candle to football, but I think I'm man enough to handle it. Particularly if you'd enjoy seeing it. By the way, you faked it pretty well at the game Saturday night."

Roxy bowed her head, graciously accepting the tribute. "I hope you fake it as well at *The Nutcracker,* then."

"You mean, not fall asleep. I'll do my damnedest. Back to Wally, though—you were saying?" Nate prompted.

"Turns out he already had the job at Bradshaw. Had it before we ever called him. Seems the city-desk editor mentioned to his wife that he'd sent a team out to interview Wally and she mentioned it to their daughter who just happens to be a buyer at Bradshaw and Sons. The daughter went to the store manager and they hired Wally over the phone while he was still eating breakfast last Monday morning."

Nate frowned and tapped his forefinger nervously against the wheel. "I don't get it. Why even agree to see us then?"

"Wally didn't get it at first, either," Roxy said. "Goldy was the one who was curious about what you and I might offer. She knew Wally wasn't interested in the type of long-term job we were proposing. As they said frequently tonight, they like to travel."

"Sounds like fun to me, too. I can afford to take you anywhere you want to go, toots," Nate claimed and slid his hand over Roxy's knee. "Where should it be?"

She covered his hand with hers. "How about if we just go home tonight?"

He most definitely liked the way she thought. "Okay, but you haven't finished my bedtime story yet. Why did Wally delay so long in telling us he wasn't interested? Was he enjoying all the attention and gifts we were showering on Goldy and him?"

"I'm sure Goldy was," Roxy said. "Wally claims he felt guilty as hell. But Goldy was determined to play Cupid and push us into each other's arms."

"Can't fault her for that," Nate said.

"Neither can I," Roxy murmured, in complete accord with him. "I'm glad it's all over, though. Aren't you?"

"All over?" he repeated. "I thought we were just beginning our adventure together."

"Life as an adventure?" Roxy said. "It is, isn't it. I'm glad my adventure coincides with yours now."

Nate was, too. Now if he could just follow his own advice and figure out a way to take enough time off to fully enjoy a love-filled life with Roxy. There was, after all, the new shop, the next issue of the catalog, the...

Epilogue

➤━━━

Nate hung around The North Pole Outlet all day Christmas Eve, anxious for the time when he could get Roxy alone. She put him to work helping customers and wasn't very surprised a month later when the inventory sheets showed very few of the remaining items had been supplied by Carrington's Christmas Catalog. Nate had pushed a lot of his own merchandise into the arms of her dazed customers during his day as an Outlet salesclerk.

They woke next to each other on Christmas morning, and later in the day, when he finally let her finish dressing for dinner at her parents', Roxy found yet another present in her Christmas stocking—a blue leather jeweler's box with an engagement ring nestled inside. Her mother and sisters were appropriately impressed with the size of the diamond when Roxy showed it off.

It was difficult choosing a wedding date, what with all the new plans they'd each made. The grand opening of Carrington's Christmas Clearance shop and the Outlet's Christmas-in-July promotion filled the better part of the summer, but they managed to tie the knot and escape on an extended honeymoon that took in both the Caymans and Maui—Goldy and Wally were pleased when they heard—squeezing in the ceremony and trip between the last day of Roxy's sale and the first of Nate's major holiday shipping dates.

Ava relished digging her teeth into planning and running TC Junior, but when Christmas rolled around the next year, she spent time at Roxy's shop, again playing executive assistant to Mr. Claus and talking to children. She then went to the Caymans herself, fell in love—for the sixth time—with a jolly, white-haired, retired novelties salesman and lured him back to work for the Triple C to fill the position Wally had rejected.

Bridget ended up running Dazzling Decor, the new offshoot of Roxy's shop, because when it came to deck the contracted halls the next year, Roxy was in no shape to be grappling with ladders. She was four-months pregnant and delegating like crazy.

Casey updated his computer security system to keep Ava and other hackers from breaking into it and found himself envying Nate's new life. He was glad that having a wife didn't keep his old buddy from attending the traditional Friday-night Adams High football games. He was surprised that Roxy came with Nate and actually seemed to enjoy the evening. Wayne Huffman, by the way, didn't manage to break the record set by Cannon-Arm Carrington, so Nate remained a legend at his alma mater for a few more years.

Wally and Goldy continued their nomadish life, flitting from one set of beaches to another, then back to their tiny house in the snowy north just before the holidays. Wally continued to play Santa, and Goldy tried her hand at matchmaking off and on but never felt quite as satisfied with the results as she was over Nate and Roxy's match.

Roxy herself was pleased with the merger of their personal lives. It had taken a forest of legal paper to keep their businesses separate, but since she frequently consulted at the Triple C and TC Junior, and Nate continued to dream up ways to improve profits at The North Pole Outlet, the careful division was only on paper.

Despite her softly rounding form, Roxy made sure the tree was decorated with all their favorite things the next Christmas. The lights twinkled softly, warming the great room in their new, larger house. A fire burned in the hearth, making the room toasty warm. She'd lit the tapers on the already set dining table. Since she hadn't found the time to learn to cook, the housekeeper she'd hired had created the culinary masterpiece in the oven. The tantalizing aroma of chicken cordon bleu fought with the scent of fresh pine and woodsmoke, making the room a sensory delight. Everything, she felt, was perfect.

Out on the breast of the new-fallen snow she could see Nate helping the neighborhood children put the final touches to a plump snowman. He would be coming in soon, his cheeks reddened from the cold, his sandy hair mussed and flyaway, thanks to the red stocking cap he'd taken to wearing in anticipation of the holidays. His eyes would soften when they fell on her, she knew, and his lips would curve in that special, heart-stoppingly precious smile. Then he would notice what she was wearing—a sprig of mistletoe in her hair, a clinging cream-and-gold Chinese robe and a welcoming smile on her lips.

This year she was really going to seduce her Santa.

* * * * *

Share in the joy of yuletide romance with brand-new stories by two of the genre's most beloved writers

DIANA PALMER
and
JOAN JOHNSTON
in

LONE ! STAR CHRISTMAS

Diana Palmer and Joan Johnston share their favorite Christmas anecdotes and personal stories in this *special hardbound edition.*

Diana Palmer delivers an irresistible spin-off of her **LONG, TALL TEXANS** series and Joan Johnston crafts an unforgettable new chapter to **HAWK'S WAY** in this wonderful keepsake edition celebrating the holiday season. So perfect for gift giving, you'll want one for yourself...and one to give to a special friend!

Available in November at your favorite retail outlet!

Only from

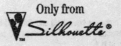

Take 4 bestselling love stories FREE

Plus get a FREE surprise gift!

Special Limited-time Offer

Mail to Silhouette Reader Service™

3010 Walden Avenue
P.O. Box 1867
Buffalo, N.Y. 14269-1867

YES! Please send me 4 free Silhouette Yours Truly™ novels and my free surprise gift. Then send me 4 brand-new novels every other month, which I will receive months before they appear in bookstores. Bill me at the low price of $2.69 each plus 25¢ delivery and applicable sales tax, if any.* That's the complete price and a savings of over 10% off the cover prices—quite a bargain! I understand that accepting the books and gift places me under no obligation ever to buy any books. I can always return a shipment and cancel at any time. Even if I never buy another book from Silhouette, the 4 free books and the surprise gift are mine to keep forever.

201 BPA AZH2

Name	(PLEASE PRINT)	
Address		Apt. No.
City	State	Zip

This offer is limited to one order per household and not valid to present Silhouette Yours Truly™ subscribers. *Terms and prices are subject to change without notice. Sales tax applicable in N.Y.

As seen on TV!
Free Gift Offer

With a Free Gift proof-of-purchase from any Silhouette® book,
you can receive a beautiful cubic zirconia pendant.

This gorgeous marquise-shaped stone is a genuine cubic
zirconia—accented by an 18" gold tone necklace.

(Approximate retail value $19.95)

Send for yours today...

compliments of ▼ *Silhouette*®

To receive your free gift, a cubic zirconia pendant, send us one original proof-of-
purchase, photocopies not accepted, from the back of any Silhouette Romance™,
Silhouette Desire®, Silhouette Special Edition®, Silhouette Intimate Moments®
or Silhouette Yours Truly™ title available at your favorite retail outlet, together with
the Free Gift Certificate, plus a check or money order for $1.65 U.S./$2.15 CAN. (do
not send cash) to cover postage and handling, payable to Silhouette Free Gift Offer.
We will send you the specified gift. Allow 6 to 8 weeks for delivery. Offer good until
December 31, 1997, or while quantities last. Offer valid in the U.S. and Canada only.

Free Gift Certificate

Name: _____

Address: _____

City: _____ State/Province: _____ Zip/Postal Code: _____

Mail this certificate, one proof-of-purchase and a check or money order for postage
and handling to: SILHOUETTE FREE GIFT OFFER 1997. In the U.S.: 3010 Walden
Avenue, P.O. Box 9077, Buffalo NY 14269-9077. In Canada: P.O. Box 613, Fort Erie,
Ontario L2Z 5X3.

FREE GIFT OFFER   084-KFD

ONE PROOF-OF-PURCHASE

To collect your fabulous FREE GIFT, a cubic zirconia pendant, you must include this
original proof-of-purchase for each gift with the properly completed Free Gift Certificate.

084-KFDR

SILHOUETTE WOMEN KNOW ROMANCE WHEN THEY SEE IT.

And they'll see it on **ROMANCE CLASSICS**, the new 24-hour TV channel devoted to romantic movies and original programs like the special **Romantically Speaking—Harlequin™ Goes Prime Time.**

Romantically Speaking—Harlequin™ Goes Prime Time introduces you to many of your favorite romance authors in a program developed exclusively for Harlequin® and Silhouette® readers.

Watch for **Romantically Speaking—Harlequin™ Goes Prime Time** beginning in the summer of 1997.

If you're not receiving ROMANCE CLASSICS, call your local cable operator or satellite provider and ask for it today!

Escape to the network of your dreams.

See Ingrid Bergman and Gregory Peck in *Spellbound* on Romance Classics.

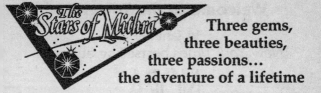

The Stars of Mithra

Three gems, three beauties, three passions... the adventure of a lifetime

SILHOUETTE·INTIMATE·MOMENTS®
brings you a thrilling new series by
New York Times bestselling author

Nora Roberts

Three mystical blue diamonds place three close friends in jeopardy...and lead them to romance.

In October
HIDDEN STAR (IM#811)
Bailey James can't remember a thing, but she knows she's in big trouble. And she desperately needs private investigator Cade Parris to help her live long enough to find out just what kind.

In December
CAPTIVE STAR (IM#823)
Cynical bounty hunter Jack Dakota and spitfire M. J. O'Leary are handcuffed together and on the run from a pair of hired killers. And Jack wants to know why—but M.J.'s not talking.

In February
SECRET STAR (IM#835)
Lieutenant Seth Buchanan's murder investigation takes a strange turn when Grace Fontaine turns up alive. But as the mystery unfolds, he soon discovers the notorious heiress is the biggest mystery of all.

Available at your favorite retail outlet.

Welcome to the Towers!

In January
New York Times bestselling author

NORA ROBERTS

takes us to the fabulous Maine coast mansion
haunted by a generations-old secret and introduces
us to the fascinating family that lives there.

Mechanic Catherine "C.C." Calhoun and hotel magnate
Trenton St. James mix like axle grease and mineral
water—until they kiss. Efficient Amanda Calhoun finds
easygoing Sloan O'Riley insufferable—and irresistible.
And they all must race to solve the mystery
surrounding a priceless hidden emerald necklace.

Catherine and Amanda

THE Calhoun Women

A special 2-in-1 edition containing
COURTING CATHERINE and A MAN FOR AMANDA.

Look for the next installment of
THE CALHOUN WOMEN with Lilah and Suzanna's
stories, coming in March 1998.

Available at your favorite retail outlet.

Silhouette®